Ella Minnow Pea

Mark Dunn is the author of more than twenty-five full-length plays. *Belles* and *Five Tellers Dancing in the Rain* have together received over 150 productions throughout the world and he has been the recipient of several national playwriting awards. He is currently playwright-in-residence with the New Jersey Repertory Company and the Community Theatre League in Williamsport, Pennsylvania. Originally from Memphis, he now lives in Greenwich Village with his wife, Mary. *Ella Minnow Pea* is his first novel.

Ella Minnow Pea

A Progressively Lipogrammatic
Epistolary Fable

Mark Dunn

Methuen

This paperback edition published in 2003 by Methuen

7 9 10 8

Copyright © 2001 by Mark Dunn

The right of Mark Dunn to be identified as author
of this work has been asserted by him in accordance with
the Copyright, Designs and Patents Act 1988

First published in the USA in 2001 by MacAdam/Cage Publishing

First published in Great Britain in 2002 by Methuen

35 Hospital Fields Road, York YO10 4DZ

A CIP catalogue record for this book is available from the British Library

ISBN 978 0 413 77295 4

Designed by Helen Ewing

Printed and bound by CPI Group (UK) Ltd, Croydon, CR0 4YY

For Mary

ACKNOWLEDGMENTS

For early support and input, the author wishes to thank Laura Atlas, Carolyn Weekley, and Phil Calbi; and Margaret Glover and Stephen Crook with the New York Public Library. Virginia Bartow, Curator of the Library's Rare Books Collection, also earns special mention for assisting the author in his research. The author is additionally indebted to Pat Walsh and David Poindexter at MacAdam/Cage who have apparently decided that playwrights can, on occasion, produce publishable novels.

epistolary (i pis´tl er ē), *adj.* 1. of or associated with letters or letter writing. 2. of, pertaining to, or consisting of letters: an *epistolary* novel.

lip•o•gram (lip´ ə gram), *n.* a written work composed of words selected so as to avoid the use of one or more letters of the alphabet.

Nol•lop (nol´ əp), *n.* a 63-square-mile autonomous island nation 21 miles southeast of Charleston, South Carolina. Established as a quasi-communal society by dispossessed southern Americans in the 1840s, the island declared its independence from the United States in 1870. Over the years the country's leadership has sought to uplift its black and white citizens through almost monastic devotion to liberal arts education and scholarship, effectively elevating language to a national art form, while relegating modern technology to the status of avoidable nuisance. Formerly Utopianna, the country's name was changed in 1904 to honor native son Nevin Nollop, the author of the popular pangram sentence *The quick brown fox jumps over the lazy dog.*

pan•gram (pan´ grem -gram), *n.* a phrase, sentence or verse composed of all the letters of the alphabet: *A quirky novel with pages of zany, jumbled lexicon.*

In the beginning was the Word.

GOSPEL OF JOHN, CHAPTER 1, VERSE 1

The wicked peon quivered,
then gazed balefully at the judges
who examined him.

ANONYMOUS TYPESETTER

ABCDEFGHIJKLMNOPQRSTUVWXYZ

The quick brown fox jumps over the lazy dog

Dear Cousin Tassie,

Thank you for the lovely postcards. I trust that you and Aunt Mittie had a pleasant trip, and that all your stateside friends and paternal relations are healthy and happy.

Much has happened during your one-month sojourn off-island. Perhaps your Village neighbors have apprised you. Or you may have glanced at one of the editions of *The Island Tribune* that have, no doubt, accumulated on your doorstep. However, I will make the safest assumption that you have yet to be offered the full account of certain crucial events of the last few days, (tucked away as you and your mother are in your quiet and rustic little corner of our island paradise) and inform you of the most critical facts pertaining to such events. You'll find it all, if nothing else, quite interesting.

On Monday, July 17, a most intriguing thing took place: one of the tiles from the top of the cenotaph at town center came loose and fell to the ground, shattering into a good many pieces. A young girl here, one Alice Butterworth, discovered the fallen tile at the base of the statue, carefully gathered up the bits and shards, and quickly conveyed them to the offices of the High Island Council. Tiny Alice delivered these fragments into the hands of Most Senior Gordon Willingham who promptly called an emergency meeting of that lofty body to glean purpose and design from this sudden and unexpected detachation.

This aforementioned gleaning – this is important.

Many in town were in attendance at this critical meeting. Olive, whom the laundress corps elected to attend as our representative/observer, given the need for a nearly full contingent of workers at the launderette on this particular day, returned much later than expected to report the have-and-say of the lengthy session, specifically with regard to the aforementioned issue and question before the Council.

I must own that we were quite ataken by the Council's initial reaction to the incident, most of us regarding it as mere happenstance. The Council, on the other hand, sought with leapdash urgency to grasp sign and signal from the loss, and having offered themselves several possible explanations, retired with all dispatch to closed-door chambers for purpose of solemn debate and disposition.

In so doing Most Senior Council Member Willingham and his four fellow counciliteurs left themselves scant room for the possibility that the tile fell simply because, after one hundred years, whatever fixant had been holding it in place could simply no longer perform its function. This explanation seemed quite the logical one to me, as well as to my fellow laundresses, with the single exception of one Lydia Threadgate who holds the Council in bloated esteem due to a past bestowal of Council-beneficence, and who would not be dissuaded by a healthy dose of our dull-brass-and-pauper's-punch brand of logic.

However, in the end, our assessments and opinions counted for (and continue to count for) precious little, and we have kept our public speculation to a minimum for fear of government reprisal, so charged with distrust and suspicion have the esteemed island elders (and elderess) become following last year's unfortunate visit by that predatory armada of land speculators from the States, harboring designs for turning our lovely, island Shangri-la into a denatured resort destination for American cruise ships.

With the Council in high conference for the succeeding forty-eight hours, the washboard brigade made at least two pilgrimages to town center, there to gaze up at the much revered cenotaph and its salt-wind-eroded statuary likeness of our most venerated Mr. Nevin Nollop – the man for whom this island nation was lovingly named – the man without whom this shifting slab of sand and palmetto would hold paltry placement in the annals of world history. We take significant pride here in town as you and your fellow villagers, no doubt, do as well, there in your green canopied hills to the north of us – pride in the man and his legacy, such legacy immortalized in tiled bandiford on the crown of the pedestal upon which his sculpted semblance stands: T-H-E Q-U-I-C-K B-R-O-W-N F-O-X J-U-M-P-S O-V-E-R T-H-E L-A-Z-Y D-O-G. Of course, now, without the tile bearing the letter "Z," the phrase "lazy dog" has become "la*y dog."

How different the world would be today if not for the sentence which the lexically-gifted Mr. Nollop issued forth! How we cherish his contribution to the English-speaking world of one short sentence that employs with minimal repetition each of the twenty-six letters of our alphabet!

The quick brown fox jumps over the lazy dog.

For this, Mr. Nollop was deserving of nothing short of Nobel. He received, instead, as you must remember from Mrs. Calliope's island history class, little recognition beyond these familiar shores. Yet remember that here we made up for the lack of global acclaim by honoring him with this imposing statue. And later the acclaim did come – posthumously, alas – but eventually and ultimately through the gratitude of the multypewritudes.

Pop volunteered to repair the tile and return it to its rightful place. His offer was summarily rejected. Rejected, as well, was an offer put forth by members of the Masons Guild to restore the entire monument to its former polished sheen and fettle, such restoration to include the careful removal and refastening of each of the thirty-four remaining century-old tiles.

But along these lines the Council would entertain no offers or suggestions whatsoever. In the words of Councilmistress La Greer Houston, "There was, without doubt, purpose to the tumble: this event constituting, in my belief, a terrestrial manifestation of Mr. Nollop's wishes. Mr. Nevin Nollop speaks to us from beyond the grave, my fellow Nollopians. We will listen with open ears, discern his intent, and follow those wishes accordingly."

On Wednesday, July 19, the Council, having gleaned and discerned, released its official verdict: the fall of the tile bearing the letter "Z" constitutes the terrestrial manifestation of an empyrean Nollopian desire, that desire most surely being that the letter "Z" should be utterly excised – fully extirpated – absolutely heave-ho'ed from our communal vocabulary!

Henceforth, use of the arguably superfluous twenty-sixth letter will be outlawed from all island speech and graphy. It appears that this is how Mr. Nollop chooses to reward the islanders who drew him and his brilliance to their collective bosom: by issuing this directive, by sitting fully upright upon his bier, as it were, and ordering us to communicate using only the twenty-five letters that remain.

And we, as his grateful servants (serving the memory of his greatness) have been called by High Council to obey. Under penalties to be determined by the aforementioned Council.

On Friday, July 21, those penalties were decided. They are as follows: to speak or write any word containing the letter "Z," or to be found in possession of any written communication containing this letter, one will receive for a first offense, a public oral reprimand either by a member of the island Law Enforcement Brigade (known with trembling affection as the L.E.B.) or by member of its civilian-auxiliary. Second offenders will be offered choice between the corporal pain of body-flogging and the public humiliation of headstock upon the public square (or in your case, the village commons). For third offense, violators will be banished from the island. Refusal to leave upon order of Council will result in death.

Death.

My dear Cousin Tassie, I could not believe what I heard – still cannot – yet it is all frighteningly true. Would that itty Alice had taken the crumbles of that terrible tile under cover of darkness to one of our masons and had it reassembled and refastened, without anyone being the wiser!

And yet, truly, there are moments – brief moments – in which I entertain the thought that perhaps there may exist some thin thread of likelihood that the Council may have correctly read the event. That as ludicrous, as preposterous as it seems, the fallen tile may indeed be communication from our most honored and revered Mr. Nollop. Nevin Nollop may, in fact, be telling us exactly what the Council singularly believes (for I understand the five members to be clearly of one mind in their belief). That having absented himself from the lives of his fellow islanders for lo these one hundred and seven years, the Great Nollop now rouses himself briefly from his eternal snooze to examine our language and our employment of it, and in so doing rouses us from our own sleepy complacency by taking this only marginally important letter from us. There is that very real, although admittedly micro-scopic, possibility, my dear cousin. For, with the exception of the use of the letter in reference to itself and its employment in the word "lazy" affixed in permanence to its partner "dog," I have, in scanning the text of my epistle to you thus far, discovered only three merest of uses: in the words "gaze," "immortalized," and "snooze." Would you have lost my meaning should I have chosen to make the substitutions, "looked," "posteritified" and "sleep"? What, my dearest Tassie, have we then lost? Very little. And please note that a new word would have been gained (posteritified) in the process! Perhaps I may actually grow to embrace this challenge as others, no doubt, are preparing to do themselves.

The edict is to take effect at the moment of midnight cusp on August 7/8. In the days remaining we are permitted to zip, zap and zoop to our blessed hearts' content. Mum, Pop and I are planning a party that evening to bid farewell to this funny little letter. I wish so much that you and Aunt Mittie could be in attendance. We will welcome in a new era. What it holds for us, I do not know, but I shall give this thing the benefit of cautious initial fealty. I leave open the slim possibility that Nollop does indeed wish it so.

With love,
Cousin Ella

Dear Cousin Ella,

New era! Posh-and-pooh! This latest development hasn't inaugurated a new era. It's only shoved us far deeper into the dungeon of Island Medievalism. We shall be wearing burlap and flour sack tomorrow, and lucubrating by candlelight because even light bulbs seem doomed now to join the official list of technological non-essentials. And now this regulation! I am bezide myself!

Your letter, I must confess, left me initially speechless, for having just returned home, neither I nor Mother was aware that any such thing had taken place! Now, hours later, I gather my thoughts together, my nerves still raw and jangled, the pen still unsteady in my trembling hand. Such an act as that presently being perpetrated on the people of this good island by our esteemed High Island Council is beyond diabolical. "Cautious initial fealty"? Have you not even considered all the consequences of losing this "funny little letter"? My friend Rachalle, who inherited our small village library with the passing of Mrs. Redfern, reminds me that with the prohibition, the reading of all books containing the unfortunate letter will have to be outlawed as well. There are, I would surmise, few, if any, volumes upon those biblio-shelves that do not contain it.

The Council, in its ridiculous wisdom, will be assigning to dust bins and community pyres centuries of the finest examples of sapience and sagacity – volume upon volume of history, literature, and thought promulgated through the medium of this cherished language of kings and knaves, scholars and clowns, to be replaced, dear Cuz, by the anemic and uninquiring ramblings of this flock of humans-become-ground-pecking-sarilla-geese, looking skyward only for evidence of approaching rain, then to seek cover, pecking and honking along the way when not following blindly the anser-herd's wooden staff, not without complaint, but certainly without measurable rebellious spirit. On second thought, my analogy seems hardly appropriate, for in the way made most significant by our circumstances, we aren't like the sarilla geese at all! For unlike our feathered neighbors who protest the tiniest importunities against their dignity, we will keep our beaks clamped tightly shut, not emitting even so much as a peep of dissatisfaction.

I am so fearful, Ella, as to where this all may lead. A silly little letter, to be sure, but I believe its theft represents something quite large and oh so frighteningly ominous. For it stands to rob us of the freedom to communicate without any manner of fetter or harness.

We are a well-educated, well-versed, and well-spoken people whom Mr. Nollop has taught to elevate language to a certain pre-eminence unmatched by our vocabu-lazy American neighbors across the sound. We are a nation of letter-writers, who, in the absence of reliable telephone service or the existence of electronic mail, have cultivated our hardship far beyond all expectation. Do you honestly believe that this same Mr. Nollop would allow his fellow islanders to see their language so diminished? Or permit diminution of the islanders themselves by extension? I cannot even conceive of it. The Council is wrong. Yet, observe that none of us will risk telling it so, for fear of the consequences. Installed for life, with complex legal procedures for official recall, copies of which will soon be disappearing from the shelves of our island libraries (if they haven't already!), this council has set us up for a most difficult period without any avenue for redress. I pray that you and I both have the strength and fortitude to weather this most devastating of island storms.

If not, God help us all.

With love,
Your cousin Tassie

PS. Neither I nor Mother will be able to attend your party on the 7th. Nollop "Im"-Pass is mired again from last week's heavy rains, and the Littoral Loop has yet to be reopened following the early summer inundata. (I would avoid the Littoral Loop, in any event, as it is, while scenic, the longest distance between two points known to man.) And please understand my unwillingness to trespass upon the Pony Expresspath; the sprinting Pony brother-couriers are Mercury-swift these days, and I would prefer that my obituary not read, "She was ingloriously run over by a fleet-footed fourteen-year-old." If I am to have any choice in the matter, I would choose a less pedestrian death, thank-you-very-much.

PPS. You will notice that with the exception of the use of the letter "Z" in the anserous term "vocabu-lazy," the affectionately familiar "Cuz," and the mischievously manufactured "bezide," the letter is employed nowhere else in this missive. My point stands on principle: to choose to use the letter if I so wish it, or to choose not to; such is my right – a right now to be eradicated by stroke of High Council pen. And with that, I cloze.

NOLLOPTON
Sunday, August 6

Dear Daughter Ella,

I am going to the hobby-shop to pick up more ceramic mix for my miniatures. I should be home in an hour or two. I have decided to narrow my latest venture from the fashioning of dissimilar vessels (the familiar tiny urns, pitchers, and amphoras which have sold so well at our recent town craft bazaars) to the exclusive molding of diminutive moonshine jugs. You might remember my telling you and your mother that Mr. McHenry of Charlotte, North Carolina, has promised to buy all the jugs I make for his American Doll House Supply Company. (And with the decline in available carpentry work around the island you know how much we can use this money.)

You may remind your mother should she return before I do that while I am out I will pick up mixed nuts and assorted beverages for tomorrow night's party. I will also bring something good for us to eat for dinner this evening.

It will not be fish.

I have apparently grown just as tired of the piscivorous diet as have you and she. Praise God for the abundance of loaves and fishes during these belt-tightening times; just leave us the loaves and take away all them fishes!

With love from your father,
Amos

Dear Cousin Tassie,

I write this letter literally minutes from the cusp of midnight. I trust that having read it, you will put quick flame to it for it will have been received after the onset of this peculiar prohibition, and I do not wish to place you or your mother in any jeopardy whatsoever, for I understand there will be no moratorium, and no lenience shown any offender over the age of seven. (Why the cutoff here, I do not know, yet any child eight and older who speaks or writes a word containing the letter "Z," it is my understanding from the proclamation, will receive the same penalty as would an adult. Children seven and younger, however, may bizz and bazz to their heart's content. Ah, to be a child again!)

I wish that you could be here. It has been an odd gathering – a warm confluence of kindred souls – yet in terms of the pervasive atmosphere, conversely, even perversely funereal. I would like to have had my dear cousin at my side as we approach the fateful stroke-and-chime. Reluctantly do we bid farewell to Mistress Z, embracing her warmly, heartily, as if determined never to let her leave our side. In spirit-most-festive do we attempt with all our intellectual muscle to name as many words as we are able from the pool of those we will soon be forbidden to use. Such a very long list we have produced – a list which will soon and sadly be curling black in the Pop-crafted salad-ceramic enlisted for its incineration.

My Uncle Zachary will henceforth go by his middle name, Isaac. His jocular carpenter-mates Buzz and Zeke ask that they now be called, respectively, Lil' Tristan and Prince Valiant-the-Comely. (Zeke is actually applying for a legal name change!)

No longer may we speak of the topaz sea which laps our breeze-kissed shores. Nor ever again describe azure-tinted horizons sheered by the violent blazes of our brilliant island sunrises.

Hundreds of words await ostracism from our functional vocabularies: waltz and fizz and squeeze and booze and frozen pizza pie, frizzy and fuzzy and dizzy and duzzy, the visualization of emphyzeema-zapped Tarzans, wheezing and sneezing, holding glazed and anodized bazookas, seized by all the bizarrities of this zany zone we call home. Dazed or zombified citizens who recognize hazardous organizations of zealots in their hazy midst, too late – too late to size down. Immobilized we iz. Minimalized. Paralyzed. Zip. Zap. ZZZZZZZZZ.

Crazy.

Crazy.

Did I say crazy?

The books have all disappeared. You were right about the books. We will have to write new ones now. But what will we say? Without the whizz that waz.

For we cannot even write of its history. Because to write *of* it, is to *write* it. And as of midnight, it becomes ineffable.

As of five seconds from now.

As of now.

The clock chimes twelve.

Goodbye * !

I have such a ghastly headache. I believe I'll go lie down now.

Love,
Your cousin Ella

ABCDEFGHIJKLMNOPQRSTUVWXY*

The quick brown fox jumps over the la*y dog

Dear Ella,

I received your letter. I read it and destroyed it. I'm sorry I couldn't be with you. As your family's parties go, I'm sure it was a memorable one, although the hovering pall must have sent folks home a little earlier than usual.

They shut the library down today. By day's end workmen had it totally boarded up. I spent much of the afternoon helping Rachalle box up items to transfer to the supply cabinets of Mother's school. Her second graders wore such heart-tugging looks of confusion when the principal confiscated all of the text books. Mother spent much of the school day in halt and stammer lest she speak the proscribed letter and find herself brought up on charges. It makes teaching so difficult, she tells me – having to spell out each word in her head before speaking it, to prevent accidental usage, while attempting to deliver a lesson without benefit of any textbook whatsoever! (Mother is having only a slightly better time of it than Mrs. Moseley who, having fallen victim to chronic aposiopesis in the morning, spent the bulk of the afternoon seated in silent defeat behind her desk, while her restless third graders improvised games of catch with a variety of show-and-tell items.)

Mother said her own pupils wanted desperately to talk about what had just occurred.

Many are forbidden by their parents to discuss the matter at home, so great is the fear of where such discussion may lead. She said that she took the coward's way out and would not permit discussion in her classroom either. It is gone, she tells the children. They must think no more of it. We must all learn to accept its departure.

"And yet, deep inside," she tells me, "I am angry and rebellious." "In my head," she tells me, "I am reciting what I recall of my niece's last letter, allowing the illegal words to baste and crisp. I cook the words, serve them up, devour them greedily. In the sanctuary of my thoughts, I am a fearless renegade. Yet in the company of the children I cringe and cower in a most depreciating way."

Mother looks at me with a face betraying all the pain she feels inside, and concludes with a whisper, "I have only shame for myself, Tassie – because of what this has turned me into, here, even in this early hour of this most senseless prohibition."

Perhaps in time, Ella, the words we have lost will fade, and we will all stop summoning them by habit, only to stamp them out like unwanted toadstools when they appear. Perhaps they will eventually disappear altogether, and the accompanying halts and stammers as well: those troublesome, maddening pauses that at present invade and punctuate through caesura all manner of discourse. Trying so desperately we all are, to be ever so careful.

It really stinks.

Even on this second day violations are mounting. Here in this tiny village, Ella, seventeen of my neighbors have already been charged with first offense. Two, in sad fact, have reached the grave level of second offense. Mr. Gregory who lives just down the lane – three milk cows he has, hardly of sufficient number to earn the title of dairy farmer. Yet he treasures the appellation, and what milk he produces is sweet and creamy. Dairy farmer and beekeeper. Owner of the largest apiary, if I am not mistaken, on the island. It is the bees that have gotten poor Mr. Gregory into trouble. For how does one describe such creatures without use of a certain outlawed letter as a matter of course? Twice, the good man has slipped up. As I write this he sits in headstock on the village commons. No one jeers, by the way. We come only to offer condolences. And to bring him drink – sweet milk from one of his own Guernseys. The day is hot, and there is no shade where he is shackled. I understand his hives will soon be destroyed, his livelihood ripped from him. For the bees speak the offending letter as their wont. They sing it into the hills, our ears ringing with its scissoresonance. Such a perturbulent distraction it is to a community attempting to follow edict with obeisance!

The other individual charged with second offense is Master William Creevy, about our age – whom Mother taught a few years previous – a riotous, rule-flouting young man for as long as I have known him. (This fact, however, never prevented me from exercising a certain youthful fondness for him; his countenance, dear Ellakins, is no strain upon young female eyes!) Willy, as it happens, does not believe in obeying laws written by madmen. And while many of us applaud his independent spirit, he is, nonetheless, one slip-word away from banishment.

I wonder what that word will be. Whatever he chooses (if choice it be), you will not see it scribbled by me within some future missive to my dear cousin, for while I share Master Creevy's contempt for the island authorities, I do not at present own his dangerous desire for insurrection.

A point made during a visit to the Village yesterday by Council Member Harton Mangrove for purpose of conform and clarification: we may not, as an alternative, use illegal words with asterisks conveniently replacing the letter of the alphabet in question. Use of such asterisk will carry the same penalty as would use of the prohibited letter itself, for one is blatant stand-in for the other with meaning wholly transparent.

Which is why you find no asterisks in this letter to you.

Pray for dear Willy Creevy. He is a mischievous, troublesome lad but undeserving of expulsion for all his mischief and trouble. Did I mention he chose flogging? A brave boy he is. But I rather suspect he's sacrificing the skin of his youthful back for naught. For the present, it is easier for us to turn away. Our repulsion, you see, will not spur us to revolt until this plague moves much closer to home.

I love you, dearest Cousin, and do so miss you. Never stop writing.

Love,
Tassie

Dear Tassie,

Today *The Tribune* published the names of fifty-eight of the sixty men, women, and children charged this week with first offense. (Two names were unpublishable due to the presence of a particular letter within.) All were speakers of banned words – words overheard upon the lanes, in schoolyards and church pews, and on the common greens. Neighbor turning in neighbor, perpetuating old grudges and grievances with this new weapon unleashed upon us by the High Island Council. The paper reported thirteen additional names of those charged with second offense. Unlike your brave Master Creevy, all have chosen headstock in lieu of the lash. Thankfully, no one has yet to receive the dreaded charge of third and final offense. At least one of the thirteen has taken the precautionary measure of taping his mouth securely shut.

Another among their number, the very publisher and editor of our *Island Tribune*, Asquith Kleeman, is contemplating a suspension of the publication of his newspaper rather than risk a final charge. For the time being he has asked that all staff members tape down a certain key on their typewriters to avoid its accidental usage. The Kleeman family, as you may know, has resided on this island for multiple generations; they were, in fact, one of the first families to settle here. Banishment for them would be both an unfortunate and landish tragedy. Just as unfortunate, though, would be the loss of our daily rag – our solitary news source (now that radio news broadcasts have been suspended).

Yesterday Mum and Pop took a long dusktide stroll along Nevin Beach. I followed not too far behind. Each of us hoped to find the peace and tranquility that usually rewards us on such quiet, contemplative walks. Yet it was not to be. The sun-kissed paradise we have cherished for all our lives has been marred by this most wretched turn of events. During such walks my parents exercise far less care in how they speak to one another than they do in conversation with others. Perhaps they should be more cautious, lest possible eavesdroppers hiding in the dune grasses report them. But for the time being they take their chances. And while they converse in soft, lovers' tones, I recite my favorite poetry with little attention to use of the forbidden letter. In the disquieting quiet, we wonder and worry, yet try to carry on some semblance of normal life. You were right about the fallout from this most absurd law. Not only does it cripple communication between islanders, it builds rock walls between hearts. As Mum holds tightly to Pop I watch them trying to feel what once came so soft and easy. Yet the growing fear coils about us in such a way that affection becomes like bud-never-bloom. The sweet scent is there – the innate desire to blossom, but the cold wind locks the bud in place.

All because of this tiny Nollop-cursed letter. I have yet to fully understand its awesome power. But I am fast learning.

Your loving cousin,
Ella

NOLLOPTON
Tuesday, August 15

Dear Goodwife Gwenette,

   You are in the tub. It isn't my wish to disturb you. I am going to town center. Prince Valiant-the-Comely says the Taylor Construction Company is a few carpenters short this week due to the grippe. I want to check with Taylor to see if he might need me tomorrow.

   I stood outside the door to the bathroom inhaling deeply the intoxicating scent of your bath beads. I would have barged right in as I used to in the old days, but you seemed all too content enjoying your "privy time." I identified all three of the tunes you were humming. They took me back a few years!

   I love you.

   I'll be home later in the afternoon. Please tell Ella that the cocktail tomatoes in the back garden require immediate harvesting; the crows are already having themselves a fine tomato salad.

Amos

NOLLOPTON
Tuesday, August 15

Dear Goodhusband Amos,

I write this on the chance that I may still be gone when you return. I will be at the market buying Cornish game hens for dinner tonight. I know how much you and Ella like them.

You think you are so smart! Now just whom do you think you're fooling? In all the years we've been married you have not forgotten a single anniversary, and I do not think you intend to start with this one. I am thus quite aware, sir, that you are not in any form, shape, or manner having a work-related conversation with Anselm Taylor (who knows to call on you if he needs you) but are, instead, even as I write this, selecting for me some appropriately commemorative gift which you have absolutely no business buying, given the precariousness of our present financial situation.

You are too, too much, Amos Minnow Pea!

With love,
Your wife of twenty-three
years to the day,
Gwenette Minnow Pea

PS. Perhaps if I chose to take another bath later this evening (while our dear daughter is working her evening shift at the launderette), you might reconsider your earlier decision about "barging right in." (Tee hee.)

Ellakins,

Young Master Creevy was sent away today. When the flogging had ended, he allegedly (I was not there.) raised his head and let spew forth a long and repetitive illicit-letter-peppered tirade against the L.E.B. officers who had administered his punishment. He was not even granted time to pack a suitcase. I will hear more of his story when his mother addresses a meeting of the Parents and Teachers Association at the Village school tomorrow night. Within an hour of this act of civil disobedience, Master Creevy was tossed upon an out-bound commercial trawler, with the summary warning that to return to Nollop would mean immediate execution.

Dear Ella, what have those fools on the Council wrought? The meeting tomorrow will allow us to vent our anger and frustration. I truly look forward to it.

Your cousin,
Tassie

Dear Tassie,

I'm eager to know how the meeting went. I wish we could speak on the phone – that phone service between town and village were reinstated; the Council continues to refer to the outage as a temporary "hurricane-related disruption" (the hurricane in question having occurred thirteen months ago). I don't believe them. I think it represents, instead, the persistent degeneration of all means by which this island may some day enter the Twentieth Century, let alone the Twenty-first. Until I can procure cups and a massive coil of string, these letters that pass between us will comprise our sole means of communication, and we should try to make the best of them. Please write as soon (and as often) as you are able.

I have some news. It is too early to know what to make of it. Or how the Council will proceed. But the possibility does exist that scales may soon fall from the eyes of the esteemed H.I.C., and they might see their way to rescinding this horrible law.

I base this belief, dear cousin, on something that has just occurred. Another tile has dropped from the cenotaph: the tile upon which was etched the letter "q" (from the word "quick"). A shopkeeper witnessed the event, and made the report. The Council went into emergency closed-door session. They may emerge in minutes, or it could be several hours. They have requested a large platter of crullers and Danish.

Love,
Ella

Dear Ella,

We had heard about the second fallen tile. We hope and pray that the Council will come to its senses on the matter.

Last night Mother and I attended a very emotional meeting of our Village's Parents and Teachers Association. Through bitter tears Babette Creevy related the details of the banishment of her son. Initially, the boy refused to go. While his father pleaded to the L.E.B. thug-uglies to ignore young William's boldly insolent hurlatory, to Willy's mother fell the difficult task of propelling her son with every ounce of maternal passion onto the boat that would serve both as his transport to permanent exile, and, paradoxically, the very instrument of his survival.

Those who witnessed the incident agreed with Babette's account of parental paralysis in the face of naked martial tyranny.

A rage burns deep within me, dear Ella, the likes of which I have never felt before. Yet collaterally a terrible fear has taken hold, robbing me of any thought of recourse. While I want to believe that the self-destruction of the second tile will bring the Exalted Quintet to its collective senses, the very real possibility exists that they could – these self-proclaimed High and Almighties – find in its demise true validation for their earlier decree and convenient justification for its subsequentia. And we sit powerless to convince them otherwise.

Please write me as soon as you know something. Mother and I feel so isolated here in the Village. While we still receive the weak signal of the limited island radio broadcasts, music is almost all that is sent up to us these days. Music without words. The station management, I assume, does not wish to examine song lyrics for words containing the outlawed letter. Besides making us all fearful, this edict has turned some among us into shameful indolents.

And if I hear "Tijuana Taxi" one more time, I am going to scream!

Your cousin,
Tassie

PS. Thanks bunches for the birthday card. And thank you for adhering to my wishes and not sending a present. One small, mischievous joy during these otherwise joyless times is finding myself a year older than you for five whole months, although nineteen feels little different from eighteen if you want the truth of it.

Dear Tassie,

No doubt, the latest edict has reached the village by post or has been tacked to the proclamata board on your Village commons. At the cusp of midnight on August 27/28, as you surely know by now, the letter "Q" will be stricken from our vocabulary as utterly and thoroughly as was its hapless predecessor.

I am incapable of any reaction beyond that which I have previously registered with you. Life, no doubt, will change little from what we now know; as luck would have it, there are simply not all that many words in the English language which claim this letter among its constituents. I am in agreement with you that as our anger against the Council grows, it has yet to exceed in potency the abject fear which invades all aspects of our readjusted lives.

There have been whispers of a Council recall; yet few, if any, among us know how to effect such a thing. Legal recall was, even prior to the incineration of the relevant statutes, a complicated process, and now, in the absence of written guidelines, remains a virtual impossibility. Others have whispered of a military coup. Yet the Island L.E.B. is handsomely paid and well provided for. I can see little to entice these officers to overthrow a government that has for the most part been both friend and ample provider, let alone an exemplar of political stability for most of its one-hundred-and-thirty-year history in the hemisphere.

We have at present no recourse but to mind our p's and bury our q's, and try our best to eke out some crumbs of normalcy from our turvied lives.

Without, I am sad to report, an island newspaper. The editor and publisher of *The Tribune*, Mr. Kleeman, has, in one grand

and glorious protest, put out his final issue, and ignoring his family's rich island heritage, voluntarily departed this cursed sandbar. But not before publishing and leafletting this town with hundreds of copies of a most special swan song edition, carrying the apt title, "The Bees' Lament" – being a delightful four-page conversation between two bees marooned upon a keeperless farm. The paper – I wish I could have sent you a copy, but destroyed it quickly after Mum and Pop and I shared a tearful laugh – contains, below the masthead and the aforementioned title, the frenetic repetition of a certain letter – four thousand, perhaps five thousand glorious times!

I do respect Mr. Kleeman for his protest, yet am disappointed by the cowardly exit. He has left this town with a yawning com-municational chasm – a great lacuna which I see no one stepping forward to fill.

I wish you could come for a visit. We have room for you here at the house, should you desire to stay for a while to seek employ-ment, or perhaps find volunteer work at our library. Happily, its doors are still open. Most of the books are gone, though – the periodicals as well. But many of the musical albums remain (without their jackets or labels). And the picture books that still reside here are quite colorful and not all that unpleasant to look at.

Give my love to your mother. (Perhaps I will see you soon?)

Your cousin,
Ella

Dear Ella,

I just may take you up on that invitation! You know how I feel living up here – so removed from things.

I look forward to visiting with Aunt Gwenette and Uncle Amos as well. I cannot wait to see your father's burgeoning collection of petite vases and jugs!

Did I mention – I have become a volunteer teaching assistant, and am helping Mother at the school. I miss the library, though, and the opportunity to read whatever I wish – whenever I so desire. I compensate for this loss by reading your letters over and over again; and Mother and I have taken to writing one another – if you can believe it – from one room to the next! She tells wonderful stories of our mothers' childhoods – all their little adventures – beachcombing for shells and driftwood, chasing sand crabs about (How cruel the two of them were as children!) and building majestic sand palaces at low tide.

I know it was necessary when I was a toddler and Father had gone away, for Mother to move us to the Village to take the teaching job, but I have never warmed to this dismal and dreary place, and I will be happy (Do not tell Mother.) to leave it and never return.

Ellakins, I must tell you: I have taken to sitting in a favorite spot on a secret hillside outside the Village to think. And dream. And watch the shapings of the clouds and feel the caress of our soft, late-summer wind wisps. Some evenings I do not return home until long after dark. Yesterday I was even naughtier than usual: I carved the dreaded letter in the bark of a lonely mimosa, carved it with a kitchen knife in great broad slashes of impertinence and had myself a delicious clandestine laugh. And I must say, it did me a world of good.

Perhaps I will take a page from your book and recite poetry.

I think sometimes of departing the island for good. But I'm not so sure I could leave Mother who seems to need me so much now. I had such lovely visits with Father's family in Savannah and Charleston, and while I felt somewhat the foreigner (My cousins say that I speak in a "funny," overly formal way, whatever this means.), I think sometimes how lovely it would be to live across the channel – like my paternal cousins. With telephones that actually work, and television and computers and books – all the books one could ever hope to read. But I wonder, as well, how much of my present disagreeableness and languor (even prior to this lexical crisis) is due to the simple fact that I have no one with whom to share my life – no companion, romantic affiliation or otherwise, save my mother. I am, I will admit, a tragic village lonely-heart at the advanced age of nineteen!

Cousin Ella, I must relate something that has happened which Mother has made me vow not to divulge. Yet I cannot honor her wishes on the matter, for I can no longer bear my concerns for her alone. Please share the following with your mother, but do share it in careful confidence. Perhaps Aunt Gwenette may advise me as to how I might be of sufficient succor to her.

You see, Mother has spoken the letter.

She has spoken the letter in the presence of her class – there, before her young pupils – and it did not go without report. One student, I am sorry to relate, took it upon himself to inform his parents, and they in turn, took it upon *themselves* to inform a representative of the villagers' volunteer auxiliary of the L.E.B. Yesterday morning Mother was brought before the faculty assembly and publicly issued citation and harsh reprimand. Before every teacher in the school was she called forth and cited with first offense, then mortifyingly reminded by captain of the auxiliary of the penalty for second offense. Mother was humiliated before colleagues whose respect she had earned and maintained for many years, word, no doubt, trickling down to her young charges whose respect, as well, is critical to the performance of her duties as their instructor.

She spoke hardly a word to me last night, and retired early. She is equally subdued this morning. I wish there were something I could do to help her. But the incident has brought her so low that I know of absolutely nothing that might elevate her spirits. I want to come to town and stay with you and Aunt Gwenette and Uncle Amos, but now must wait until Mother's emotional state has improved.

I believe that I will write a letter to the boy's parents to find out exactly what purpose was served in reporting Mother, given the enormous difficulty island teachers face in their efforts to avoid just such a slip as the one my mother experienced. A different law should be passed for teachers, if you ask me. There should be a special waiver or accommodation extended not only to seven-year-olds but also to those who are asked to instruct them.

I will write again soon. Please do not mention in your next letter to Mother what I have just told you. She will discuss it with you, I am certain, when she is ready. When the shame of it has sufficiently ebbed.

Love,
Your cousin Tassie

PS. I did not tell you how the slip occurred. She was teaching arithmetic and made mention of a sum of eggs. Twelve eggs to be exact. And described them using a word no longer at our disposal. A right and proper word in times gone by. How DOES, IN any fair and logical way, the Council expect us – all of us – not to make such a simple and innocent slip every now and then!

Dear Niece,

I am so sorry to hear from Ella of my sister's recent misfortune. The odds were that it would happen sooner or later. She must try doubly hard to be more careful in what she says to those students of hers. Little rabbits have big ears. Especially in light of the fact that as of Monday we will be pressed to avoid yet another clutch of outlawed words. Your mother and my beloved sister, I must say, will look not at all becoming in wooden headstock!

As for how to assist her in her present state of despondency, I can offer no advice but that you continue to be the kind and understanding daughter I know you are, and give her the time she needs to find her way back to her former sunny disposition. I know that sometimes it takes your dear mother a while to recover from episodes of abashment – especially ones so public. But I assure you, recover she will. She is intrinsically resilient. We all are.

We have no party planned for Sunday night. We will let the midnight chime usher in this new micro-era in our island history with neither comment nor incident. Amos and I will, no doubt, be fast asleep when the fateful hour arrives. (I'm not sure of Ella's plans for that evening.) Before retiring, though, I shall turn to my dear husband and say, "Today we queried, questioned, and inquired. Promise me that come tomorrow, we will not stop asking why." And Amos, being Amos, will chuckle and perhaps respond, "We'll never stop asking, dear. Now to sleep. Quiet, dear. Quiet, quiet. To sleep."

Your aunt loves you,
Gwenette

Ella here: I plan to be asleep as well. I am working longer hours at the launderette now. All of these emigrating islanders are so insistent upon packing only the most spanking clean clothes into their trunks and suitcases. I do not blame them, but it is exhausting work!

ABCDEFGHIJKLMNOP*RSTUVWXY*

The *uick brown fox jumps over the la*y dog

Dear Mr. & Mrs. Towgate,

I am Tassie Purcy, daughter of Mrs. Mittie Purcy, your son Timmy's teacher. I am writing to ask why you felt it necessary to report my mother's slip of the tongue to the island authorities. Mistakes will be made by all of us during these trying times, and it is my belief that latitude should be extended to those like my mother who are employed in professions in which one is called upon to speak for long, wearying periods and through a wide swath of subject areas.

I believe there was an element of cruelty in what you did, the source of which I now seek your assistance in dowsing. My mother has done nothing to harm any member of your family, and has been especially attentive and helpful to your son Timmy who is a restless student and a slow learner.

This whole incident has distressed her greatly. Please explain why it was necessary.

Sincerely,
Tassie Purcy

Dear Miss Purcy,

We are sorry that the performance of our civic duty has resulted in distress to your mother. We assure you that it was not our intent to single her out for any specific harm, nor was the report made in retaliation for any wrong which we feel was done to our son Timmy or to any other member of our village clan by your mother.

We believe, Miss Purcy, as you obviously do not, that there is full cause and merit to the statutes recently passed by the Island Council. We believe, further, that Nollop does indeed speak to us from his place of eternal rest, through the manipulation of the tiles upon his hallowed cenotaph, and that the Council serves only as his collective interpreter. If I understand correctly, it is your belief that the two restrictions recently imposed upon the residents of this island have been fashioned for some purpose to which Nollop is not even party. A fairly blasphemous position you hold, if I may be so bold. If such were the case, would not the Council exempt *itself* from such restrictions? And yet, I know, as you must, that our Council members ask nothing of us that they are not willing to ask of themselves.

My wife Georgeanne and I are happy to see members of the Island Council continue to serve as sole diviners of the will of Nollop. (For who should know better than the most sage among us?) Perhaps you and your mother fancy yourselves standing upon the same high plain. Know this: such a self-delusional position can only serve to isolate you from the rest of this community at a time when we ought to be meeting our challenges in full union and concert.

Why do we follow, without misgiving, the will of Nollop?

Simply because without him this island would be a shallow shell, an empty conch compared to what it has, in fact, become: a beautiful, sandy-shored haven of enchantment and delishmerelle. And without whom the world would never have been given the foxy-dog sentence we have all grown to cherish (but which, naturally, until instructed otherwise, we must no longer speak or write in its entirety).

Your mother should essay to be more careful in the future.

Sincerely,
Nash Towgate

Dear Tassie Purcy,

I must insert this note with my husband's letter, and state, first, that I am in full accord with the sentiments contained therein. I sincerely believe, as do several who have joined me for bi-weekly talk group sessions, that Nollop, as one who put great emphasis upon the word, is now attempting to pry us away from our traditional heavipendence on linguistic orthodoxy. Through this challenge, he hopes to move us away from lexical discourse as we now know it, and toward the day in which we can relate to one another in sweet pureplicity through the taciteries of the heart. Brilliant in life – now brilliant eternal in his conveyances from Beyond!

With all cordiality,
Georgeanne Towgate

PS. If you and your mother wish to join our talk groups you would be most welcome; we gather in my front parlor each Tuesday and Thursday evening at 7:30.

PPS. As an additional demonstration that there is absolutely no ill will being extended to your mother by anyone within the Towgate household, please accept, as well, my invitation to the both of you to join me and other villagers-artistically-inclined for our bi-monthly Monday night tempera bees. (Until last week these were weekly gatherings, but too many among our membership wished to be released to attend the newly established Village Women's Humming Chorus.)

Dear Sister Gwennnetttte:

Robbed of two letters, I now chooooose to overuuuse the twenty-four which remaaaain.

I hope you and Amos are well. I haven't been feeeeeeeling myself lately. Tassie worrrrrrries about me. Sheee shouldn't. I will bounce back as I always do do do do do do do do do do do.

Love,
Your Sister Mittieeeeeeeeeee

Dear Ms. Purcy,

My name is Nathaniel Warren. I am a Master's candidate in history and sociology at the University of Georgia. I am also publisher and editor of a new academic journal *Nollopiana* with publication of its first issue slated for later this fall. As you might guess, my journal is exclusively devoted to your island, its people, and its unusual history.

Last week I was contacted by someone you know: a young man by the name of William Creevy. Mr. Creevy had heard of my publication and wondered if I might like to write about his recent expulsion. He is presently without income and says he could benefit from any compensation I might offer. I agreed, but soon came to see that another more broadly encompassing article begs to be written.

Through my lifelong interest in Nollop I have gained a level of familiarity with your country that has until now been matched by only a handful of Americans and Nollopian expatriates. That interest has fueled a desire to learn as much as I can about your island, and to share what I learn with others. In light of recent events, this mission has become much easier. Lately, Americans have started to take much closer notice of their tiny neighbor to the southeast. In fact, I estimate that if these strange edicts erupting from your high council continue, the whole world may soon be demonstrating a rubbernecking interest in your plight. I have already made a number of advanced subscription sales to residents of the coastal tidelands whose number now includes a growing community of Nollopian émigrés.

Now to my reason for writing: I would like to come to Nollop for a lengthy visit, for purposes of investigating this odd, unprecedented political and social crisis in which you now find yourself embroiled. Since my interest in Nollop has been hidden to some degree by the veil of academia, my name and face may not be known to the Council, and so my application for short-term visa may stand a chance for approval. I know that the Council has, since Statute 24-37, refused entry to all American journalists and scholars. (All the news of the latest goings-on has come from those who have involuntarily – or in an increasing number of cases, voluntarily – left the island.) As an added pre-caution I will assume, with your permission, the role of "old friend of the family." Mr. Creevy reports that you and your daughter have remained in Council favor, and so I'm hopeful that such a visit won't raise governmental objections.

I know that I am asking much from you; I am, after all, a total stranger to the two of you. (And yet from Mr. Creevy's descriptions of you both, I do feel that I know you somewhat. I understand that some of Mr. Creevy's happiest childhood moments were spent in your company – with you as his second grade teacher and your daughter Natassa as his middle school English tutor.)

I will certainly understand if you have reservations, and if those reservations prevent you from allowing me to stay. (If this turns out to be the case I trust that you will divulge to no one the fact that I approached you in this regard.) But if you feel as many of your fellow islanders do, that the actions of the Council should be brought to the light of public scrutiny with my earnest little journal serving as appropriate vehicle, perhaps your convictions might outweigh any misgivings you may have about the reason for and the manner of my visit.

I look forward to your response.

Sincerely,
Nate Warren

Dear Mr. Warren,

I have discussed your petition with my daughter Tassie. She has allayed my minor concerns, and so I am able to hereby welcome you to our home as "good old friend of the family." I look forward to hearing if your application for visa will be approved. Please let us know if there is anything we can do to help.

Best wishes,
Mittie Purcy

Dear Cousin Ella,

Mother is better, buoyed somewhat by the strangest letter we received last week, from a gentleman named Nate Warren who publishes a journal about Nollop. He wants to write an article for American readership on the Council's actions of late, and for this purpose has asked if he might come to stay with Mother and me. Mother immediately wrote him back to say yes, by all means. I have never known her to act so hastily in any regard!

I must say that I am rather looking forward to the young man's visit.

With love,
Your cousin Tassie

Dear Tassie,

I am excited to learn of your soon-to-be house-guest. Anything to boost Aunt Mittie's foundering spirits, and yours as well!

Perhaps, by now, you have heard of the tragic public flogging of the Rasmussen family – all six members whipped like misbehaving canines on the public green as was their choice following the soon to be infamous Daffy and Donald affair.

Their offense? Each member in deliberate provocation of the High Island Council had marched single file into last Tuesday's open session wearing cartoon masks and making loud duck sounds – sounds which any sentient Nollopian knows by now are forbidden – while holding aloft large cardboard containers of a certain recently outlawed brand of American oatmeal.

As the Rasmussens were being manacled by members of the L.E.B., Council Member Willingham asked for the reason behind such a flagrant flouting of the "clear and unambiguous" law against use of the seventeenth letter – a flouting made all the more "pernicious" by the enthusiastic abandon with which it was embraced. The head of the Rasmussen household, Charles Rasmussen, Sr., a clothing merchant here in town, (I bought a lovely powder blue lace partete from his store just last month.) responded, "It was actually my children's idea. They are very fond of this letter and felt a protest against its removal from island discourse was very much in order. My wife and I agree. We also wish to be flogged in the presence of as many town residents as choose to be in attendance. And if this produces no outcry – especially the laying of leather tassel upon the youthful backs of my nine-year-old twin daughters Becka and Henrietta – then please trundle us without delay from this island of cringe and cowardice, for we no longer wish to belong to such a despicable confederacy of spinal-defectives."

And so Mum and Pop and I stood and watched the harrowing and loathsome sight of children being ritually beaten, and the commensurately disturbing picture of frightened onlookers – "the town baa-baas," as Pop has taken to calling our dear neighbors – doing what they do oh so very well, and that is: absolutely nothing. Lifting not even the proverbial finger to remove these high council bastinado-bendiced buffoons from their pinnacle of abusive power, nor doing anything otherwise to stop or decelerate their efforts. Watched these Nollopimpotents, Mum and Pop and I did, as they stood in willful immotility. And as we absorbed, in full, the lamentable scene being played out before us, we found ourselves entertaining identical thoughts – concretious thoughts of retaliation and the ultimate reclamation of a society so disturbingly transmogrified.

A first meeting to be held in our home a week from tomorrow under the guise of Pop's twice-monthly poker game. To plot and plan our insurrection – our nascent underground movement to restore a full twenty-six-letter alphabet to the people – deserving or not – of this, our presently polluted island home!

Even as this morning – in the early predawn darkness one Creighton O'Looley was discovered attempting to replace a tile newly fallen. He was apprehended and is being held without bond for attempting to circumvent this most recent misconstrual of all-holy decree from the great and omniscient Nollop.

J. –

It could have been worse.

But J!

As you might say: Jumpin' Jehoshaphat!

Love you. Love to your mother.

Ella

Dear Ms. Purcy,

My application for visa has been approved and I will be arriving Monday, September 18, at Pier Four in Nollopton on the 4:12 Walmart supply boat. If it isn't convenient for you or your daughter to meet me, I will find my own way up to your home in Nollopville. (It shouldn't be difficult. I spent my childhood studying maps of your island.) As I understand the internal mainway is mired this time of year, don't expect me until late.

I have just received word about the loss of the tile containing the letter "J" and do not wish to wait until I see you to share important news. Chemists here in Georgia who have obtained smuggled chips from the two earlier fallen tiles have just completed an exhaustive battery of chemical analyses on the fixative that has held the tiles in place for the last hundred years. Their assessment is that the glue – a strange compound not familiar to them – glue which also oddly, and we now know impractically served as a substitute for simple, durable cement – has calcified to the point of ineffectual granule and powder. Within months, perhaps even weeks, all of the tiles currently mounted on the cenotaph will become similarly loosened and fall to the ground. The chemists doubt that within a year's time there will be even a single tile left affixed to the monument. Should your council continue along its present course, the outcome will be too dire even to contemplate. Here I am telling you nothing you don't already know.

(I am, as you can also imagine, fast losing my academic objectivity; word of the Rasmussens' ordeal reached us this morning.)

While researching the series of articles I now plan to write on the Council's recent actions and the tangible effects those actions are having upon the residents of Nollop, I seek, in addition to your hospitality and safe cover, assistance from you in reaching that one member of the Council you feel most open to reading the chemists' report, and making a case for a reversal of these apocalyptic directives.

It is, I believe, well worth a try.

Sincerely,
Nate Warren

Dear Ella,

Most wonderful news. Mr. Warren, who will be arriving on the 18th, is coming to our rescue! I know it's foolish to put stock in any promises of assistance (and while I hope that your underground meetings prove independently fruitful, I cannot count on them – forgive my blunt honesty here – and must parcel my optimism in such a way as to best contribute to the state of my emotional health) but I am nonetheless encouraged by the following: Warren arrives bearing more than simply suitcase and notebook. He brings, as well, the results of chemical analyses performed on slivers of the errant tiles – analyses which prove beyond doubt and wanton denial that the tiles are falling for the simple reason that they can longer hold themselves to the bandiford. It is as elementary as that. Nollop is not God. Nollop is silent. We must respect that silence and make our decisions and judgments based upon science and fact and simple old-fashioned common sense – a commodity absent for too long from those in governmental elevatia, where its employ would do us all much good.

I seek your assistance, dearest cousin, in determining which of the pious five would be most open to reading Mr. Warren's report. I think, perhaps, it should be Mr. Lyttle. He has always seemed to me the least moronic of the bunch. Indeed, if I am not mistaken, Mother voted for the man many years ago for this very reason.

Rush me in tomorrow morning's post, dear Cousin, your much anticipated opinion in the matter. And good luck with tonight's meeting. Please don't interpret my lack of active endorsement as a dismissal of your family's admirable efforts. I'm afraid I am becoming more and more the selective cynic. Thankfully, now and then I do see glimmers of hope. And Mr. Warren has just unveiled such a glimmer.

I am looking forward to my upcoming visit with you and Aunt Gwenette and Uncle Amos. Let me know when it would be most convenient for me to come down.

Mother sends her love.
Tassie

Greetings, Nollopians,

It has come time for the Council to make its position clear and direct with regard to the issue of the fallen tiles. Indeed, our last three executive sessions were devoted exclusively to this task. The product of those sessions is this letter which we now post to every family on the island in an effort to bring us to common mind on this, the most pressing matter ever brought before our people. It is a matter with which each member of this body has tuss-and-tangled. Late into the night have we searched our souls, into the wee smalls have we plumbed our hearts with profound and inten-sured moral rectilitude. Because a formidable duty has been charged to us, an overtitious ask-me-now posed, yea posited, which we cannot in good conscience ignore. And in the answer, in the noble venture of compliance, our mission now comes to encompass the putting forth to all of you, the good people of this proud and independent island nation, the reasons behind what at times must seem a harsh and unwavering capitulation to the wishes of Almighty Nollop. This we do. We do willingly; we do dutifully.

Some, including those malcontents and apostates who have since departed our shores, might wish to modify the word "wishes" in the previous paragraph by the term "perceived." As if everything passed down to you from Council Assembly has been based upon supposition – upon meandering hypothesis and amorphous conjecture.

It is none of these things.

The signs have been presented to us, and while it took us a while to ascertain the desired course rising from their assignment, we now, we are happy to say, and with only temporary delay, securely grasp and freely endorse without temperage these pathfinders dropped, literally, at our feet.

For those of you who desire explication, we offer the following ten salients:

1. Nollop was a man of words.
2. We are a people of words.
3. All that we are, we owe to Nollop.
4. His will be done.
5. We have become unfortunate victims of our own complacency.
6. Complacency is a destructive force, capable of ending through invidious stagnationality all that is good which we have created for ourselves here.
7. The falling tiles can represent only one thing: a challenge – a summons to bettering our lot in the face of such deleterious complacency, and in the concomitant presence of false contentment and rank self-indulgence.
8. There is no room for alternative interpretation.
9. Interpretation of events in any other way represents heresy.
10. Heretics will be punished, as was, for example, Mr. Nollop's saucy stenographer, who was cashiered for flippantly announcing to her employer the ease with which she could, herself, create such a sentence as his.

Those of you who see undue cruelty in the penalties meted out for speaking or writing the forbidden letters should make note of the following three points:

1. Adhering to the commandments of Nollop leaves no room for fear of punishment or forfeiture. (He who walks in the light has no reason to fear the darkness.)
2. There is no such thing as accident or misspeak, only grossly under-applied discoursal perspicacity, with unguarded exposure to distractional digression. (A lighted path is clear. There is no reason, save mischief or inattention, to stray into the darkness.)

3. The severity of punishment is an irrelevant issue, given the opportunity to avoid punishment altogether. (Keep to the path to avoid what is promised to be a broken and jagged shoulder.)

Returning to the saucy secretary: she was given fair warning by Nollop that her insubordinate speech would not be tolerated. That one of such intellectual inferiority could ever in a lifetime duplicate the work of Nollop was unfathomable, her claim hypercomical. Nollop said as much, even challenged the pert stenographer to come up with a sentence of her own measuring thirty-five letters or less and containing all of the letters of the alphabet.

She tried.

She failed.

In fact, the best that she could muster was a short anecdote about an imaginary animal park in which the occupants revolted by exchanging their stripes and spots. It ran precisely 289 letters.

She used the word *yak* three times.

The secretary, we might further add, was never able to come up with a sentence matching Nollop's because it simply cannot be done. This is what has given Nollop his preeminence. Omnipotent. Omniscient. Omniglorious.

Praise Nollop.

And honor his wishes by removing "J" with jubilation.

Sincerely,
Your High Council
Gordon Willingham
La Greer Houston
Harton Mangrove
Rederick Lyttle
A. Plastman

ABCDEFGHI*KLMNOP*RSTUVWXY*

The *uick brown fox *umps over the la*y dog

Dear Mr. Minnow Pea,

I am in receipt of your letter regarding my order of miniature moonshine vessels. (Note that I have no interest in violating your Island Council's three recent statutes regarding alphabetical elision, and so we will continue to refer to the vessels as, simply, vessels.)

Given the marketability of your previous consignments, the 50 figure is much too low. Please deliver to my warehouse double that amount by December 1 – in time for the Christmas market – and I will pay you an additional $5.00 per vessel, with a bonus of $550.00 for the effort. (Please note: all payment will be in American dollars and not in Nollopian Nevins. Given the instability of your national currency, I see no reason for you to oppose this arrangement.)

I look forward to hearing if you will be able to meet the order, and look forward, as well, to many years of doing business with such a talented artisan.

With all best wishes,
Charles Ray McHenry

NOLLOPVILLE
Monday, September 11

Dear Mother,

I have finished the wash, hung all the clothes out to dry, and gone down to the shore to find starfish for my collection. Abby says the tide brought in a number of small ones this morning. You were so sweet to make crab cakes last night. Perhaps you will make them again next week for Mr. Warren. No one can resist your scrumptious crab cakes.

Come down later and spend some time with me. I miss the old you. Can I say that? You've changed so much over the last few weeks. I do worry about you.

We can make do without this new letter, as we have without the other two. It should not be so hard. You will see.

Love,
Tassie

My dear friend Agnes,

Thank you so much for the cookies. You sent far too many, regardless of the state of my emotional health. I will share them with Tassie and with some of the neighborhood children, but even then, I shall still have cookies to spare!

You are a good and kind friend. I have treasured your friendship as far back as I can remember, and will always do so.

Love,
Mittie

Dear Mittie,

I am recalling the day we met. We were all of four! How is it possible to remember so far back? Perhaps because I counted you as special friend from the very moment our mothers plopped us down on the seesaw together.

I bake my raisin-pecan cookies, darling Mittie, because there is little else I can do. What is happening here to you and me, to our families and friends – it frightens me so that I sometimes find myself standing for long periods of time in the middle of my kitchen – much like a statue – much like that infernal statue of Mr. Nollop – immobile, unable to do anything except return by cursed rote to the baking of my cookies. And this I do, often late into the night.

Do you think I am losing my mind?

When I bake, I do not have to speak. When I bake, I do not have to make sense of anything except the ingredients summoned by memory that I have laid out in front of me. Sometimes the children offer to help, but I do not accept. This is something best done alone. Something I do well. One of the few things I can actually *do*.

So eat them. Eat them all. I will bake more.

It is what I do. All I *can* do.

Love,
Your friend,
Agnes

NOLLOPVILLE
Wednesday, September 13

Dear Mrs. Purcy,

I feel that I owe you and your daughter Tassie further explanation for my rather odd behavior when you came into my market yesterday. In a nutshell: my wife has left me. Donna has taken our two girls and is moving to the States. I could not convince her to stay.

I have, obviously, been a little distracted lately and simply wasn't paying attention. I should never have rung up your baisley cheddar three times. You have shopped at my market for years, and surely must remember nothing like this having happened before.

Perhaps I am wrestling needlessly with a decision that has already been made; it would be impossible for me to move to the States with Donna. My livelihood – what there is left of it – is here in Nollop. My home is here. (In addition to which I own about fifty acres north of the Village in the glades, currently undeveloped, on which I have hopes of some day building a small retirement community for myself and others.) I am angry that all we have come to value, perhaps even take for granted, is being ripped from us – one tile at a time.

And I will not stand for it.

My brother Clay, whom you may know – I believe you trade at his confectionery – believes that the falling tiles do not in any sense indicate a desire on the part of the very late Mr. Nollop to remove these letters from our language. He believes, in fact, the exact opposite. That this is Nollop's way of encouraging us to use these special letters more than ever before. They are being singled out for this purpose and this purpose alone.

He is founding a movement.

I was as of a moment ago interrupted by one of my customers.

She reports that the tile containing the letter "D" has fallen. I don't think this is mere rumor.

God save this doomsaken little island!

Sincerely,
Rory Cummels

Dear Mr. Cummels,

(May I call you Rory?)

I do not fault you for your behavior on Tuesday. We are all on edge, some of us more so than others. I am so sorry to hear that your wife and daughters have left, and I truly understand how difficult it would be for you to emigrate as well. Your corner market has been a welcome fixture in the Village, and it would be a terrible loss to see it close.

This is not, perhaps, the appropriate time, but I should like to invite you to take coffee with me when an occasion proves convenient. I should like to hear more of your brother's movement and your own opinion of it. I should like, as well, to seek your advice on other matters.

The news of "D" is, alas, all too true. I dare not even contemplate the attendant ramifications.

With all best wishes,
Mittie Purcy

NOLLOPVILLE
Friday, September 15

Dear Mrs. Purcy,

Thank you for your kind invitation. I would be delighted to meet you for any beverage of your choosing. At the risk of being too forthcoming with regard to the details of my present situation I should state that my wife has left me not only in the proximital sense, but in the marital sense as well. Divorce, I'm afraid, is imminent.

I look forward to seeing you soon (in some milieu other than my store).

Sincerely,
Rory Cummels

Hello Neighbor,

You are invited to attend a showing of "Surf of Dreams," a collection of seascapes and sky studies by Georgeanne Towgate.

Where: The Towgate front lawn.

When: Sunday, September 17.

Bring your checkbook and a smile.

Please! Silent, pantomimical bids only.

In the land of no "D," silent reverence is king.

Georgeanne Towgate

[scribbled note at the bottom]

Mother, I found this taped to the front door. Does the name sound familiar? It's that awful woman who reported your classroom slip. Know a good rainmaker?

Tassie

Dear Cousin Tassie,

Much to tell and little time to tell it as the afternoon post goes out in less than forty-five minutes.

Last evening's meeting was a pyrrhic success. Pyrrhic in that we had to turn more away than we would have liked, lest we betray, by our sheer numbers, the purpose behind our assemblage. And because word seemed to have spread among many whom we did not know, there was no discussion per se – only promises to meet again in smaller numbers, to ensure that knowledge of our secret confabettes would not spread to those with power to see us disbanded before we have even gotten started.

Funny, isn't it, dear Cousin, to have a meeting, and an enthusiastically attended one at that – in which nothing gets discussed! Ah, but the things that went unsaid! And the things that shall be said and done when we feel safer and more secure in our gatherings.

You are right that Mr. Lyttle is the likeliest candidate from among the Penta-priests to see the chemists' report, although I don't trust any of the five to open their minds even a scintilla to such a pound-logical explanation for the tumbling of the tiles. And Lyttle *has* been somewhat the taciturn rubber-stamper of late. But perhaps it is because he has yet to be offered opportunity to stand on his own two callused, septuagenarian feet, thereupon to manipulate agenda for his own purposes – one of those purposes being his very own political survival.

Am I not the cocky one! No, dear Cousin, I don't think the tide is turning. The tide which washes the shores of this beleaguered island can be depended upon to follow the moon's directives from now until the death of the planet, but lovely storm tides – beautiful hurricane-force, beach-battering, dune grass-deracinating gales do strike our beaches now and then, and leave change in their wake. Perhaps we are about to see such a storm. We will proceed on hope, comfixed in one mind and purpose upon these elite, self-deluded flayers of children.

Come down as soon as you like. We miss your smile!

As we will sorely miss the loss of "D" effective as of midnight tonight. (Have you not noticed the product of my decision to dribble this dreadful diatribe with as many uses of the doomed fourth letter as possible?) Only idiots, dear Cousin, or certifiable madmen would assign divine purpose to ridding ourselves of the tools not only with which to address Heaven itself (Henceforth "Deity" and "Divinity" and even the word "God" will be outlawed. The Council makes the following substitutional suggestions: "Omnigreatness" and "Screnity.") but also of the ability as of midnight to discuss with anything but great difficulty everything that has occurred in the sanctified past. In taking "ed" away (Goodbye, Ed!), the most useful tool to express the past tense in the English language, we are being robbed of great chunks of our very history. This constitutes, in my opinion, a significant crime, an egregious sin, and one humongolacity of a daunting challenge.

But then, according to Nollop, that which challenges us also makes us stronger – better able to serve his memory, better able to serve one another in service of his memory, better able to serve ourselves in service of one another in service of his memory.

Sometimes I find myself laughing until I begin to choke.

Yipes! The Pony-post cometh!

Love,
Ella

(And gooDbye for the last time!)

NOLLOPTON
Friday, September 15

Dear Nollop Dweller:

Many of you have visited the Council office over the last several days, voicing concern over how best to express in the absence of the letter "D" – which leaves us at midnight tonight – each of the seven days of the week. This is a valid concern, but not one that should in any way threaten daily discourse. For instead of the calendrical terms Monday, Tuesday and so forth, we cheerfully offer the following surrogates. Use them freely and often, for their use honors us all.

For Sunday, please use *Sunshine*

For Monday, please use *Monty*

For Tuesday, please use *Toes*

For Wednesday, please use *Wetty*

For Thursday, please use *Thurby*

For Friday, please use *Fribs*

For Saturday, please use *Satto-gatto*

Parents: you may wish to help your children absorb these new words by turning the process into a game of some sort, simple flash cards also constituting a tried and efficient course.

Sincerely,
Hamilton Ferguson
Chief Secretary
High Island Council

ABC*EFGHI*KLMNOP*RSTUVWXY*

The *uick brown fox *umps over the la*y *og

Ella,

Mr. Warren is here. I wasn't aware that he was so young! Perhaps he only looks young. I chose not to ask his age so as not to embarrass him. Maybe twenty-four. No more than twenty-six, I think.

He is also very attractive. He parts his hair in the center, picking up on the style of the local boys. I can tell he wants to fit in. I can tell that he wishes not to arouse anyone's suspicion.

He is single, as well – at least from what I have been able to learn. He was happy to show me pictures of his mother, his cocker spaniel, even his eight-year-young niece, but no beautiful fiancée, thank heaven!

I'm not sure why I am acting the schoolgirl. Perhaps because it has been so long since we've given welcome to such an interesting visitor. I know what you must be thinking. But I can assure you: the purpose of Nate's visit is *not* to fall in love with me. Yet in my heart of hearts, I must confess: I simply cannot stop myself from the inevitable "what if"!

He got in last night, by the way.

Have I written that he's witty? Clever to near-fault, it turns out. Not to mention the fact that he speaks with such a mellifluous Savannah-honey-voice that I come close to simply melting away each time he opens his mouth!

I must confess, as well, to being still in the thrall of two full glasses of Sonoma Cabernet. I write you – glancing at the clock near my cot – at one in the a.m. Sleepy, I know I ought to be, but I am not!

I must also relate how taken Mother is with our new house-guest. For his part, Mr. Warren has been most open to our smile-accompanying, eager-to-please hospitality – reciprocating our courtesies with southern-tangy flattery, in couplet with sweet masculine grace.

He will be staying with us for a week or so before traveling to your neck of the forest to meet with Mr. Lyttle. If I am lucky, his trip to town will concomitate perfectly with my own trip to see my most favorite cousin.

Tomorrow I shall wake, thereupon to wish none of this were put to paper, but by then it will be too late, for this letter is going into the corner mailbox as soon as I can throw on a robe to venture out. What a lovely time we have spent this evening, Sweet Ella, even without the use of the four illegal letters.

(I must own to a slippage on occasion; there was slippage from each of us as the evening wore on, our tongues becoming looser; it was almost impossible not to stumble in light of the intoxicating circumstances. But we were lucky in that when such a mis-speak took place, there were no ears pressing themselves against the portals or fenesters to overhear.)

I trust, as always, the safe, non-intercept passage of this letter. For while arguable is the possibility that Nollop speaks to us post mortem – sans mortar as it were – the one thing that isn't contestable, that rings with pure alloyless truth, is the last thing that left our venerable vocabularian's mouth prior to his expiration: "Love one another, push the perimeter of this glorious language. Lastly, please show proper courtesy; open not your neighbor's mail." (You may recall that this was a rare pet peeve of Mr. Nollop's.)

Love,
Tassie

Ella,

I beg you to ignore that last letter. I was in a state of shameful inebriation. Mr. Warren is a nice man. That is all. A nice man. I am near mortification!

Love,
Tassie

My loving sister Gwenette,

I cannot teach. Without that grammatical unifier. It is impossible. I plan to resign tomorrow.

Semicolons are simply not an option. These youngsters are only seven! Young people of such age can't fathom semicolons!

Nor can I employ an "or" when I want the other one – the one that brings together, not separates.

My brain throbs. I have a hangover. Far too much wine last night.

The wine. Plus the loss of that grammatical unifier. It is all too much.

Forgive me for my weakness.

Love,
Your sister Mittie

Throbbing Sister Mittie,

Still you are luckier to be in the village. Eighteen families were sent away this morning. Many of the members I knew. Losing the first three letters was relatively easy in comparison to this most recent banishment.

Slips of the tongue. Slips of the pen. All over town people hesitate, stammer, fumble for ways to express themselves, grip-grasping about for linguistic concoctions to serve the simplest of purposes. Receiving no easy purchase.

I go to the baker's. I point. We all point. We collapse upon our mattresses at the close of each evening, there to feel … feel … utterly, wholly diminished.

There. I now happily enlist in the "first offense club." It feels exhilarating! You know I cannot allow you to be a member of any club to which I cannot belong. I will show a copy of this letter to one of our local authorities.

I will receive my official censure.

We shall be sisters-true as always.

Love,
Gwenette

Mrs. Minnow Pea:

We appreciate your coming to us with a copy of your letter to your sister, but it was unnecessary. Your offense was known to us even before the letter's receipt by your sister. Effective as of September 15 the primary responsibility of our isle's new assistant chief postal inspector has been to scan all post for use of illegal letters of the alphabet, then to make nightly reports to the Council. A report has been put on file on your behalf, your official sentence to be forthwith in issuance.

Forty-eight hours hence you will present yourself to an officer of the L.E.B. at Town Center, there to choose between cephalo-stock or public flogging, as your use of the letter-combination at the close of the tertiary paragraph in your epistle to your sister contains not one employment of an illegum, but two. Perhaps you were unaware. This is no excuse (especially in light of the fact that your choice of this letter-combination was attributable to flagrant provocation).

We might note – to allay certain fears – that the assistant chief postal inspector may not upon Council behest report the content of anything he sees in the performance of his responsibilities. His task is merely to seek instances of illicitabetical activities. Ours continues to be a free, open society. There will be no censures or prosecutions for exercising one's free speech rights in service to the laws of this nation, even if those rights entail criticism of the High Council. You may be certain of no violation of Nollop's terminal-cot wishes when we say that all letters, all parcels that the inspector opens which are not violative will be promptly put to seal, then sent on their way. As a further assurance of the guarantee of your constitutional right to privacy, please note: the assistant chief postal inspector is an imbecile-savant from France. English is a foreign language he has yet to master.

Sincerely,
Hamilton Ferguson
Chief Secretary
Office of High Isle Council

Tassie,

I cannot believe it. Neither can Pop. What was Mum thinking? We are encouraging her to choose cephalo-stock. I will not allow any mother of mine to submit to the lash.

With love,
Ella

Mittie,

I cannot imagine that they are looking at our mail without ulterior motives. Henceforth, I encourage you not to censor your text, but to give serious thought to using the Tisbee-Cohane Cross-Isle Courier Service for all letters you wish to post to me. They are as fast as the Pony Brothers Express; most importantly, their gypsy operation more often skirts the attention of the postal inspectors. I will use them as well. I will also encourage the girls to employ their services. The only potential unpleasantness I can foresee in making the switch will be an occasional stench upon the envelope, owing to the fact that the Tisbee-Cohane Cross-Isle Courier Service is run by employees of the Tisbee-Cohane Septic Evacuators.

Still, though, I think it worth it. We now live in an official police state, be sure of it.

I chose cephalo-stock, you will be happy to hear. (Following much pressure by family members.) It was not so traumatic as one might think. There were a number of others in similar straits. Many of the families brought bulging picnic baskets. There was also a lovely fish fry with hush puppies (your favorite!), buttery corn-on-the-cob, mouth-watering tomato slices ... Also, the singing of tuneful Gullah folk songs. It was, I must profess, one of the nicest afternoons I remember having spent in some time. Amos was even able to sell a few of his miniature spittoons.

Two chose whipping. Valiantly, the men took their lashes – later wearing the crimson stripes as emblems of honor. You may know these two; they are from the Village – members of a sect which believes that Nollop's wishes have been put to gross misinterpretation. Rather than shunning the letters per Council proclamation, they urge the opposite to the extreme. The problem with this position, as refreshing as it seems, is the unfortunate result that naturally follows the putting of such belief into practice.

Must go now to massage the crick in my stiff neck.

By the way, this is the sixth anniversary of Amos's recovery. Not so much as a beer in all these years in spite of the sort of stressful circumstances that might prompt even Carrie Nation to imbibe (naturally using her hatchet as a resourceful bottle opener!).

Love,
Your sister Gwenette

Ella,

Last night, I woke from a horrible nightmare in which I saw myself sitting beneath the cenotaph as another tile fell to earth. The tile came to rest facing up. It was an "I." I woke screaming. Mother spent the next few minutes trying to convince me that the chances of this happening were slim – that so far, Nollop has been most helpful to us by keeping all vowels firmly in place. Hearing my scream, Nate came into the room to comfort me as well.

"Then you believe in the power of Nollop?" I put to Mother.

Mother shook "no," but then gave this response: "Here is what I believe: if Nollop actually exists – in spirit form, of course – then perhaps it is for some positive purpose – perhaps even the interposing of a finish to all this insanity emanating from Council Chambers."

Now Nate was smiling. "The fable of Nollop has won acolytic support in the Purcy house of all places!"

Mother: "Mere supposition, Mr. Warren. I'm only saying *if* Nollop exists …"

Now a bigger smile from Nate, then: "So why thinkest thou, he hasn't chosen thus far to take 'heavenly' retribution against this cretinous council of yours?"

My turn now: "Because he is waiting for the right moment?"

Nate shook no, while grinning his biggest grin of all. "You want the truth of what I think? Here's the nutshell: Nollop when he was alive was pure charlatan. A veritable con man. Phenomenally successful in pulling the wool over the eyes of 35,000 naivetés, ripe for the pulling. If he exists at all as manipulating eternal spirit, I see no reason for his not being of the selfsame ilk."

"Humbug terrestrial, humbug everlasting?" Nate was beginning to make sense.

"Humbug, yes, as well as simply not a very nice man. Listen up, my pretty Purcy postulators …"

(Nate was becoming a bit familiar; this was not a problem for Mother or for me!)

"… your council was built on power-lust. Nollop's whole life was a construct not only of such lust for power, but of an unnatural craving for outright worship. Yet the man was without any merit, any virtue – holy or otherwise – whatsoever. Look at what befell his secretary. For that matter, look at what befell nearly everyone he met. All those instances of truth, fairness, humanitarianism, altruism: pure mythology. Perhaps worse than mythology: Nollop has become your Baal."

"Baal?" This from Mother, although I was taken back as well.

"There's 'Biblical' for you."

My shiver was obvious.

Nate was finishing up now: "Allow me, finally, to offer up this arresting little trenchancy: given a few weeks, I, or either of you – most anyone on this isle for that matter – might learn how truly easy it is for one to create a sentence of length matching Nollop's – perhaps one even shorter. In fact, this may be our ultimate salvation."

Mother fell silent, I as well.

Sweet Ella, broach this at your next meeting. I am curious to learn the response it receives.

Love,
Tassie

Tassie,

Intriguing as Nate's proposition is (I will present it as you suggest.), an even more curious event has taken place. An "O" has fallen. One of the four "O"s. (The last appearance in the vulpine-canine sentence.) The Council has gone into emergency session. What meaning to assign to loss of a letter whose removal leaves three companions still extant?

I carry a mischievous grin upon my lips. How will they glean? Whatever will be their ruling this time, now that Nollop has become strangely obtuse? We await their pronouncement. In the meanwhile, I eagerly await the arrival of my cousin, along with her new companion, Nate.

Love,
Ella

My sweet Mittie,

This will be my last letter to you. I can write no more. Writing has never been an easy task for me, even prior to the loss of the fourth letter. It now takes a large part of my wakeful hours trying to make intelligible contact with those I love. I haven't your schooling nor your facility with language. It compels all the mental energy I can summon simply to communicate orally with Cooney, not to mention the young ones.

I no longer bake cookies.

In your last letter you wrote of how unhappy you are. My hours are spent in similar melancholy. I am speaking less. There have been two slip-ups. The next will surely result in my banishment. I cannot leave my Cooney, my Sabina, my Geryl, my Ursula, as well as the one whose birth name we may never again speak. (She has chosen "Bathsheba" as a substitute, but it will take some time for me to become wholly comfortable with it.)

My sweet Mittie, it is strange, so terribly strange how taxing it has become for me to speak, to write without these four illegal letters, but especially without the fourth. I cannot see how, given the loss of one letter more, I will be able to remain among those I love, for surely will I misstep. So I have chosen to stop talking, to stop writing altogether.

Perhaps we will see each other soon. That is, if you are still here. Many, as you well know, are leaving us. Perhaps I may come to your house for a visit. (Cooney loves it there near the water. He says there is no better fishing on the isle than from the village pier near your home.) We will not speak, we two, but I eagerly expect to pore with you in warm silence over our musty high school annuals, as well as those fox-worn nature scrap-books we spent several beautiful summers lovingly compiling.

Pray for me, sweet Mittie. Banishment for me would mean my very extermination!

Love,
Your Agnes

NOLLOPTON
Thurby, September 28

To Agnes Prather,

We write to inform you that in your letter to one Mittie Purcy on September 27, you chose to use in the line beginning: "Banishment for me ..." a letter-combination containing one of the four graphemes presently unavailable for your use per Council Statute 28-42.

Please make note that this, for you, constitutes offense number three. It will be necessary for you to report to Barkation Pier Number Seven at 9:30 a.m. on Satto-gatto, September 30 for permanent expulsion. You may bring two suitcases. We will permit, also, one hatbox.

Sincerely,
Hamilton Ferguson
Chief Secretary High Isle Council

Sister Mittie,

I have news. We may continue to use the letter "O" until such time as its brothers choose to fall. (Notice that I prefer not to attribute the recurrent plunges to the Almighty Nollop!) However, the High Council asks that we cut usage of the letter by twenty-five percent. I am curious to know how they plan to police this.

Tassie is here! She arrives as I write these very lines. I have not seen my favorite niece – can you believe it? – in almost six months. Nate accompanies her. He is everything that has been written about him. Polite. Very nice looking. I will wish him luck in his meeting with Mr. Lyttle tomorrow.

A little not-so-positive news: Amos has been caught in offense number two. In last night's poker game. It was such a foolish mistake. It might have gone without report except that Morton who owes him money chose to employ outright extortion against poor, hapless Amos. Amos's preference was for not playing along. Imagine the effrontery: Morton attempting to ignore the offense in exchange for clearance of a rather large financial obligation. Amos thought, of course, that Morton was bluffing. Unfortunately, in this particular game, it turns out, Morton was not.

I say foolish, because any competent contemporary poker player knows that this game is rife with lexical pitfalls. Best to play in wary silence. Yet Amos wasn't silent. In fact, Amos, thanks to chugging back four bottles of stout lager, was anything *but* silent. May I repeat an important part of this last statement? Four. Bottles. Yes, Amos has fallen totally off the wagon. Moreover, the wagon has all but run over him.

The wages for the topple were high: by concentrating a little too much on refraining from use of the fourth letter, he was to employ by careless miscalculation the tantamountifically perilous tenth letter of the alphabet. Thank Screnity the suit in his possession was hearts or he might be on a boat Satto-gatto morning. (King, Consort, Knave. Knave! I thought all poker players were in agreement on these new royal appellations!)

Love,
Gwenette

Mother,

We are here. It was a pleasant trip.

Nate is preparing to meet with Mr. Lyttle. Aunt Gwenette is herself preparing for her big meeting tomorrow night. She will invite Nate to speak to the group. Uncle Amos agrees that this is a wise move. Nate has several things of importance to tell the members of this refreshingly subversive sub-terra group. It is all very exciting. I think we are on the brink – things possibly beginning to turn in our favor. In spite of the loss of the new tile. You will hear soon. Not to worry. It is one we can easily spare: "K." My preference: the loss of another "O," but we can certainly live with this.

I love you, Mother. (Please Heavenly Nollop, spare "V" till the last, so that I may continue to profess my affection for my precious mamah!)

Tassie

PS. The statutes come with greater alacrity. The latest official elision takes place at 12:00 on the Satto-Sunshine cusp!

PPS. I am falling in love with Nate. There was a kiss – a passionate kiss – on the trip to town.

It took me completely by surprise. Kkkkkiss me again, Nate, while I may still speak of it!

My loving Tassie,

I must tell you of something nice that has taken place. I was sent an invitation by Mr. Rory Cummels who you will remember is the owner of the market in our village. To come to his house for coffee – for a pleasant neighborly chat. Rory hasn't the trouble most here in Nollopville have in carrying on conversation without the usual stuttering stoppages that seem to penetrate every verbal exchange I engage in in these trying times. It seems a gift, his knowing instantly which letter combinations to use to bypass the verboten ones.

In turn, I gain an easiness, a level of public comfort I haven't felt for some time. He is cheerful, but not without his own tales of sorrow. His family has left him. It is now official. He cannot follow, as he is in possession not only of a fairly profitable business (With the closing of McNulty's Greengrocer, you're probably aware, his will be the last grocerateria in the Village!) but other real property as well. To simply walk away from such an investment – this can only be financially catastrophic! There is also, relating to his wife, the matter of alienation of affection; his marriage is in its last hobbling months.

I believe that Rory likes me, Tassie. He seems to truly appreciate my company. I want to see more of him. I believe he seeks the same of me.

Finally! A bright ray in all the murk. I am not feeling even an ounce of concern over the loss of "K." "K" may go. The two of us will learn to accept its loss.

You are probably at this point, examining this letter with utter stupefaction. Has your gloomy mother taken leave of all her senses?

No. I'm only allowing myself a little happiness while I am still able.

You know, as I, that time is running out.

Love,
Mother

Mother,

I am very happy for you. Meeting Mr. Cummels is a positive thing; I am sure of it. I worry that there is no one looking out for you now that I am here in town. I'll worry less knowing that the two of you may become close.

Nate has met with Council Member Lyttle. There is much to relate.

Nate began the meeting with a formal presentation. Lyttle gave it his close attention. In the presentation Nate built his (in my opinion, extremely substantial) case for the reason we, along with a number of prominent American chemists, believe the tiles to be falling. When it was over, Lyttle sat back in his chair, let his eyes close in momentary rumination, then gave his response: "It may be true. It may all very well be true."

Then, silence. A long silence which I knew from Nate's expression left him slightly uneasy.

Eventually, Lyttle spoke again: "I may be alone within the Council in leaving open the possibility that this theory – this careful interpretation of events as you present it to me – may very well ring true. Nevertheless, young man, it is still important for me to see more compelling proof"– Nate was obviously upset by this response, but kept his temper: "But you have the lab reports, sir. They're right in front of you. What more is necessary?"

"You've given me the scientific reason for why the tiles are falling, Mr. Warren. But might not Nollop be working *through* the science? Have you ever thought of this? The science, in point of fact, actually serving his specific purposes. Therefore, that of which I must have positive proof – the single fact that I must know for certain is that the Great Nollop isn't working *at all*!"

"But *what* proof? I can't raise the man from the grave to ask him point blank!"

"Still – "

Nate thought. Lyttle thought. Then a smile from my Nate. I knew. I knew from the look on his face what was to come next.

"You venerate Nollop for one reason, Mr. Lyttle. One reason only."

A tip of the noggin from Lyttle. "The sentence. That awe-striking sentence which graces our national cenotaph."

Nate went on: "But what if it turns out that Nollop wasn't the only man capable of cobbling such a sentence?"

"But he was."

"But what if there have been others?"

"There have been no others, Mr. Warren. We are fairly certain of this."

"Fairly, but not absolutely. Please, Mr. Lyttle, hear me out. What if it were possible for someone other than Nollop to come up with such a sentence, in say – hmmm, what might be an appropriate – "

Lyttle wasn't one to let others finish *their* sentences: "If I were to give you until the last setting sun, Mr. Warren, it cannot – simply *will* not happen. Why, it's pure, utter futility!"

"But – "

"Your point isn't a complex one, Mr. Warren. What you are saying is that if there exists such a person with such a gift, why, we might have to place that special person right up there with Nollop. On the very same plane. Is that not the thrust of your argument?"

"If he or she is successful, well, naturally we – "

"Is this a challenge, Mr. Warren?"

"Might you welcome such a challenge, Mr. Lyttle?"

"I may not welcome it. I might, however, in proper fairness, entertain it."

"Then I'll make it official. It's a challenge. Will you take it to the Council?"

"A sentence of thirty-five letters or less." Then a crinkle – no, an elaborate furrow to Lyttle's hoary brow. He was thinking. Intense, all important, history-making thoughts. "No. It must be conclusive. Thirty-five letters isn't conclusive. I suggest thirty-three, no – thirty-*two* letters."

"Thirty-two letters?"

"That's correct."

"But that leaves a mere six for replication. Six!"

"That's my offer. Take it or leave it."

"How long will you give us, Mr. Lyttle? Remembering, of course, that Nollop spent all of his youth creating *his* sentence."

"Well, I certainly won't allow more than a few weeks. Especially with all the help you will be receiving. You'll have until November 16 – Nollop's birth anniversary. Remember, as well, that this offer must still win approval by the Council."

Nate thought this fair. The two men shook on it.

At the sub-terra meeting tonight the challenge will be put to all present. We hope to relay it throughout the nation. (Please cast it about the Village on our behalf.)

We will cross our fingers that the Council approves. We'll know nothing until after the council session tomorrow morning.

With this most encouraging news I'll close, but not without saying farewell to my favorite breakfast cereal. (You will, of course, remember to throw out the Special K, yes, Mother?)

I love you.
Tassie

ABC*EFGHI**LMNOP*RSTUVWXY*

The *uic* brown fox *umps over the la*y *og

Mother,

So much to tell, so little time to tell it. Those who were present at last night's meeting have chosen to embrace the challenge with absolute relish. The prospect of actually being able to control the outcome of this ghastly assault on our collective spirit, let alone our very humanity, by turning this offensive upon its cephalus, has sent some among our sub-terra movement to heights of unencompassable ecstasy. The best news of all: the Council is in full agreement with the challenge (It was official as of this morning.), so secure they seem to be in this asinine "unassailable" position of theirs. We approach the ramparts ourselves commensurably secure. High noon awaits.

At first Nate thought that he might get news to a computer programmer with whom he is familiar – a former college roommate in Orangeburg, South Carolina, who he is certain can crunch the letters, to, in effect, assemble the necessary sentence within a matter of hours. But if the Council were to learn that the sentence was put together by means of artificial intelligence, it might wholly thwart our primary purpose, this being to show that some other human – not Nollop – most certainly not an electronic computing apparatus – was able to come up with the obligatory sentence containing all twenty-six letters of the alphabet using only thirty-two letters in its execution. So he chose to expel that thought without pause. What it will come to will be this: one of us will create it: a sentence to surpass that of Holy Nollop. One of us shall, I am certain, achieve the goal of burying the myth of Nollop forever. For the next forty-six sun-to-suns, this will be our *raison*.

Mine, yours, even your gentleman companion Rory who

perhaps is still unaware of the other legislation to come out of this morning's session: "All property left in state of non-occupation through emigrantal vacatement will be given over to confiscatory oversight by the Council, then borne to official annexation into Nollopian tax-exempt ecclesiastical boroughs, thus falling within clear parameters of Council owner-management." Even as things exist now, Councilman Harton Mangrove is in the process of moving with his family onto the estate of Georgie Boonswang, whose fish cannery after closure, was left in similar circumstance of non-occupation (but not without "proper" ownership, courtesy of egregious title-alteration!). Other Council members seem to be contemplating similar confiscatory moves.

I must close now to return to my labors with the "group": Nate, Ella, Aunt Gwenette, Uncle Amos, each of us in pursuit of the magical, temporarily elusive sentence that shall result in our emancipation – to be sure, our very salvation! Albeit a more corporal form of salvation. Our souls, though, are another matter altogether. To apportion worshipful allegiance to both our Heavenly Omnigreatness, as well as to Nollop-the-mortal-marvel has become so very tiresome.

One Supreme Being is enough for me. I much prefer the former to the latter.

Love,
Your Tassie

My Tassie,

I am watching you through the pane. You sit at the table scribbling – scribbling, then erasing, biting, chewing the unfortunate pencil's extremity as you contemplate. I share your chore. I might be your portico twin, in perch upon this fresco-chaise, performing same, were it not for glimpsing you through the glass. Such a beguiling sight – your long auburn tresses falling as cataract in shimmering filamentous pool upon the table top, gathering in swirl upon your note paper – obscuring? framing? your toil. I must return to my own mental labors. But you have given me pleasant momentary respite.

My beautiful Tassie, I so love you.

Nate

Mittie, my gentlenurse,

I appreciate so much the thermos of pullet soup you sent over. You will be happy to hear that I am feeling much better this morning. When I am stronger I am most eager to see you in some other capacity than nurse. (Not that you haven't been an excellent caregiver.)

I trust that you are still well, that you haven't caught this nasty flu circulating through the Village. These are not opportune times for any of us to be ill. There is much that we must accomplish.

I myself, in spite of the flu, have spent the better part of two nights coming up with a sentence containing all twenty-six letters of the alphabet of a length of less than fifty letters – forty-nine to be exact. I was hoping to surprise you with one of far more impressive brevity, but shall be happy with my initial effort. Still, though, it will not fit the ultimate bill; therefore, in concert with so many other villagers whose lamps burn late into the night, I will push on, whittling my count away.

Accompanying this letter is a note brought to you by Eugenia, a little neighbor girl whom you may have seen playing on the lawn next to mine. She is all of seven, but the perfect age to write my sentences for me for purpose of conveying them to you, so that you may monitor my progress. I expect you will employ a youngster yourself in similar fashion so that I may learn of your progress, as well. (What a convenient loophole the not-always-farseeing Council has given us by the exemption from these laws of little ones such as sweet, cooperative Eugenia. The only problem exists in getting across to her through a series of elaborate gestures or comic pointings my intent. For there really is no other legal avenue but pantomime to communicate my full meaning to her. Then through her, to you. Bright youngsters are a precious asset in Nollopville in these troublesome times.)

Sincerely,
Rory

A quick move by the enemy
will jeopardize six fine gun boats.

Rory,

Your sentence is so much better (also shorter) than mine! I am almost reluctant to show my efforts to you. But a promise is a promise. I am in collusion with a boy by the name of Wesley, son of the Noonans who own Noonan's Florist. Wesley is very popular; I must share his services with four of my neighbors!

I am expecting a letter from Tassie. She will report how things are going in town. Rumor has it that someone – a professor with the university, I believe – has himself come in below 48. If this is true, it is very encouraging, is it not?

Sincerely,
Your Mittie

Back in my quaint garden,
jaunty zinnias vie with flaunting phlox.

Mother,

Two letters fell last night. "F." Then another "O." The Council plans to excise "F" as of twelve o'timepiece on the Thurby/Fribs cusp. I assume they will also instruct us now to shave consumption of the letter "O" by fifty percent.

There is at present fantastic support for what we in town have come to call, "Enterprise Thirty-two." Still, the Council laughs at us. They taunt the little ones who write our sentences, who transport them between our houses. They gather in reverent, worshipful circles beneath the cenotaph to sing praises to Nollop. It is a stomach-churning sight even forgetting the abuses the Council is currently inflicting upon the remaining inhabitants of this isle. This recent confiscation of property is a clear violation of the National Constitution, yet Councilwoman Houston says we are now in an "extraconstitutional crisis" which calls for "extraconstitutional measures." The Council is preparing for that moment in which language, as it once was, ceases to exist. As far as I can tell, such preparation involves chiefly the feathering of the counciliteurs' own nests.

We pray to our own Omnipresence that the final moment never arrives. We're getting closer. Professor Mannheim has given us a sentence with 47 letters. It is a simple sentence which the chosen six-year-young courier put to scription in no time at all.

Nate isn't sleeping. I am after him to complete his first article for *Nollopiana*, but he seems bent on assisting with Enterprise Thirty-two. It is an obsession. The fear is gone, though. This noble movement has given us all a special courage.

I miss you. Be well. I hope to see you soon, when all of this is over.

Love,
Tassie

John Prady, give me a
black walnut box of quite small size.

Tassie,

You were not at home when they came. Three L.E.B. officers in possession of papers. Papers with my name on them. Your Cousin Ella was there, though. Your aunt, your uncle as well. They will tell you more this evening.

I write this from the Office of Corrections at Town Center. I must remain here until the chief magistrate is able to see me. I have a strong sense as to what this is about.

Apparently, someone has become aware of my publication. Information about my whereabouts has brought them straight to me.

If I am to be stolen from this Isle, stolen from you, it will be my own fault, through not using an alias when I came over. Will you ever forgive me, Tassie?

Will I ever see you again?

If you are giving any thought to coming with me, I will not allow it. You must stay to fight, because I cannot. This is not an act of gallantry, of heroism on my part. I am only being practical. I want you to be practical too. To contribute where I now cannot.

Be sure of it, my Tassie – that when the battle is won, we will be together again. Enterprise Thirty-two will be a success. It will be our happy fate, you'll see.

Your cousin, your aunt, your uncle – they all agree with me. Even your mother up in the Village, I am sure, if it were put to her.

I will try to contact you before they put me on the boat. If I miss that opportunity, please write. Continue to write. You cannot let them stop you.

Soon we may all have to learn Hawaiian.

With love,
Nate

Mother,

Nate is no longer with us. I enclose a copy of the letter he sent me. He was gone before I even got to Town Center. Banishment was swift. Swift, I believe, because of his alien status.

I am at a terrible loss, Mother – one I cannot even begin to articulate. Were there all twenty-six letters available for my use, my ability to translate my feelings, my thoughts of Nate to this page might still be put to supreme test.

"F" leaves us tonight. I haven't even the strength to curse those beasts with that epithet you taught me never to say. It's pointless at this point, anyway.

So long, "F." So long, my sweet Nate. I will miss you. Ferociously so.

Love,
Tassie

ABC*E*GHI**LMNOP*RSTUVWXY*

The *uic* brown *ox *umps over the la*y **g

Ribs, October 13

Nollopians,

Many have come to us to learn whether or not, given the latest alphabetical prohibition, employing tetra/penta class numbers as numerals (e.g. 4; 5; 45; 54; 5,445; 554,554,455 etc.) is still allowable. It is. (As you can plainly see.) Using numbers will always be permissible. There are no numbers in the vulpine-canine sentence. Only letters.

Sincerely,
Hamilton
Executive Secretary
High Council

Tassie,

Violation number two this morning, this hapless Ribs the Thirteenth! I was caught in the act, very near our house – right there at the piscimonger's booth on the pier while purchasing shrimp! (It was my plan to surprise Rory with a special gumbo supper to honor his birth-anniversary.) I witlessly put to use a grapheme which I have been – at least up to now – abstaining with relative ease:

"Boil-seasoning with that, Mrs. Mittie?"

"Not this time, Xenia. I'm preparing gumbo."

Then a most curious stare. I'm sure I won't be able to relate to you with any great success this woman's expression. But I'll try, nonetheless, (because it was such a strange mixture): surprise, slight anxiety, momentary consternation, then over-whelming, saucer-eye panic!

I began to stammer: "What is it? What have I –"

It then became obvious. In an eye bat. All this time – in my brain – never having seen her name written out, I was misspelling it. You see, Xenia's name began not with an X, but with the other letter – the one that brought in this whole reprehensible era! Hers was, obviously, the legal spelling. Hence, my culpability.

This woman isn't a stranger to me, Tassie. I am no stranger to her. There is twenty-year amity between us. This is why I am so sure that she wasn't the one to report the violation. It was the other woman. The one in line with me wearing the worn-out tunic with all the paint splotches. Georgeanne Towgate. The ever-present, honor-bent Georgeanne Towgate!

I'm sure that she was the one whose ears got it all. My suspicion was met by a smile – a sinister simper, twisting her saliva-moist, overly rubilious lips as she apparently thought it all through – especially how important it was to bring this glaring violation to the Council's attention as soon as possible.

My thoughts were spinning at that moment as well: giving serious contemplation to pushing this Mary Cassatt aspirant – now my veritable nemesister – right over the railing. Straightway into the heaving sea. What a pharisaic, vigilante witch! The nerve – to report me – not once, but twice!

Not being one to waste time about such things, Mrs. Towgate, I'm certain, brought in her eyewitness report within minutes; by early evening your poor mother was in ignominious cephalo-strait.

The opportunity was mine to silence the witch in perpetuity. I let it go. I am an ignoble poltroon!

Sincerely,
Your ignoble poltroon Mother

Aunt Mittie,

Tassie gave me your letter. I am so sorry. What a moronic way to spell one's name! Give me permission; I will happily terminate Mrs. Towgate, saving you the trouble.

Enterprise Thirty-two has hit a wall at 47. Instructor Mannheim with the university, in alliance with his tireless pupils, assures us that they will soon breach barrier 44. But I am not so sure. Many others here in town, though, seem to have given up. Pop is beginning to believe it to be an impossibility – this thirty-two-letter grail ("chimera" he calls it) we all pursue. But I am not in agreement with those who own this opinion.

So many long-time isle inhabitants are now gone. Most are expulsion victims, but some are no longer with us simply because they choose not to live in such a hostile, inhospitable place. It is no place to thrive, Aunt Mittie – no place at all to raise young ones, to be even marginally happy.

Mother worries about you with Tassie not there. (Especially given what you mention in your last letter.) Is the gentleman Rory being proper helpmate/protector? It gives her solace when she recalls your mentioning his ease with language – the way he seems to clearly embrace the challenges inherent in communication with restriction. Ah, that we might all ultimately rise to such challenges.

Tassie is well – heart-ailing, but otherwise well. We will not permit you to worry about her. She is writing to Nate as much as she can. There are no guarantees that her letters are getting through to him in the States; she can only trust that those to whom she passes them to smuggle out, with proper payment, will honor their contractual agreement.

By the way, her epistles must still be written with all alphabetical restrictions intact, lest interception bring them to the L.E.B., the result being Tassie's own banishment. (Although, I must say she is in a better position than most, without even a single violation to her name.) This is an important point; recently, several on their way to Pier Seven (then on to the States) wrote parting letters without employing the necessary caution with respect to current alphabetical restrictions, only to have the recipients themselves brought up on charges! Remember, as well, that L.E.B. thugs are still wont to engage in spot home searches, hoping to turn up anything containing the illicitabeticals. One cannot be too wary; last Thurby, a woman who lives near us was brought into L.E.B. Precinct 2. The charge: an unthought-through grocery list seen by a thug, there on her icebox.

Pop is staying out late, coming home with a pungent alcohol smell about him. (I am not eager to tell you this, but Mother will not allow me to engage her on the topic). 48 hours ago he was put on notice by his wholesaler that U.S.-Nollop business transactions were moving to hiatal suspension. Were Pop to continue to create his miniatures, especially those popular moonshine vessels, he will have to emigrate to the U.S. Which means we will have to go too. I am sorry to say, Aunt Mittie, that I was not sympathetic. Because this obviously means leaving my eighteen-year home here, who can say how long? Leaving all that I cherish. Leaving Tassie. Leaving my sweet Aunt Mittie.

There have been reports that Nollop expatriates are having a rough time in the States, are very much "at sea" in American society, in cultural isolation as it were – unable to melt into the proverbial American melting pot. It will be the same with us, I am certain. As long as we are there we will live as outcasts.

I will tell Pop that we will live on my washerwoman's income, on our meager savings, until this crisis comes to a close. Then, as expatriates begin to return home, house construction will surely begin anew, carpenters such as Pop naturally obtaining ample employment in the process.

But let us say this never occurs. That the crisis continues. Because we cannot move below 47! Because the best brains at the university – the best brains in the nation cannot move us anywhere near 32 by November 16! What then?

It is late. Pop has yet to come home. Tassie sits writing letters to Nate – letters he may never see.

The gnawing apprehension has come again.

Help me, sweet Aunt Mittie, not to give in to it.

Love,
Your niece Ella

Ella,

I cannot help you. Not now. Please tell Tassie: Rory is gone. It began this way: brash Council representatives, upon reaching his northern acreage, gave him papers that gave them authority to appropriate his property. No reason was given other than: "It is the Council's wish."

"Meaning it isn't Nollop's wish?" was Rory's angry response.

"On the contrary. The Council serves *only* Nollop. By extension, then, Mr. Cummels, whatever laws the Council passes, are laws which by their nature must certainly have met with Nollop's approval."

"But I can't possibly see how stealing another man's property meets with Nollop's approval."

"The reasons are strictly ecclesiastical in nature, Mr. Cummels. Perhaps the Council wishes to erect a tabernacle on this site."

Rory was seething, his countenance nearly vermilion in hue. My worry that moment was that poor Rory might have a coronary arrest!

"A tabernacle – a temple – you actually mean – you actually mean a house in which to worship Nollop?"

"That is correct."

"But what about the Supreme Being we presently choose to worship?"

"There is no other Supreme Being but Nollop."

"Repeat that statement, sir. Please. I want Mrs. Purcy to hear it."

I was then brought over as close witness.

The Council representative – his voice: even, treacly polite – gave his response again, with slight elaboration: "Mr. Cummels, it is the Council's earnest conviction that there is no other Supreme

Being but Almighty Nollop. None whatsoever. Praise Nollop. Nollop eternal."

At this point, Rory lost all control. Now, Rory isn't a very religious man – at least I never thought so. But he became at that moment positively apoplectic – moving to assault the representative with everything available to him in his verbal arsenal, utterly without restraint – letting loose with a veritable, vituperative salvo – nothing printable here. Expulsion was complete within an hour's time, as an outgoing ship was set to leave at precisely the moment Rory was brought to the pier.

There was a cursory exchange between us – an impotent attempt at a chin-up bon voyage replete with the now customary, almost prosaic parting anguish. A moment later he was gone. As the ship was pulling away, Rory gave the store hasty mention. It is mine now. I will try to run it as best I can, preserving solvency until his return. Given this provision: he actually returns.

That is, given this provision as well: the Council chooses not to turn the little store into yet another Nollopian church. A church to bring a smile to that corpsal countenance we all must revere, or else. We have seen the "or else." It no longer scares me. The lamp will burn late tonight. We will best 47. Our battle may ultimately result in our extinction, but we will win at least this small success. Less than 47. It can be. Nollop was able in 35. Let us remember, as well, that Nollop was an imbecile.

With love,
Your Aunt Mittie

Nate,

I'm not sure this letter will reach you, though I pray the contrary. Time is running out. We cannot go below 47. As much as we try – that is, those who are still trying. I'm aware that some are still laboring at the university. Mother writes to Cousin Ella that she continues her own moiling over the alphabet up in the Village. But the mass exit has nonetheless begun. Townspeople. Villagers.

As three more tiles have given plunge. All in one evening. Two "E"s, then a "B."

We have one "E" remaining. The "B" may be a blessing. Other possibilities might have been more troublesome. (Yet as I peruse what I have written up to now, I note six "B"s in the last two sentences!) Who, then, can ever be sure about such a thing? At this point, losing *any* letter can only be problematic.

We have come to a travailious time, Nate. Mother's Rory is gone. Mother, Aunt Gwenette, Uncle Amos – each has one violation to spare, then banishment. I am growing so weary with that term. "Banishment." You hear it all over. In urgent whispers; in hopeless cries. Companion to the listless, vacant stares – stares belonging to those who live in resignation to the grimmest possible outcome, all but put to seal. "Banishment." We say the term. We write the term. Believing somehow that in 36 hours, it surely will *not* be gone. That somehow the cavalry will come to our rescue!

But *we* are our own cavalry. The only cavalry there is. Whose horses seem in permanent hobble status!

"Banishment": the next banishment victim! To become one more invisiblinguista. The 4000th, 5000th such victim? Is anyone counting? Perhaps Nollop? Expunging each entry in his Heavenly Lexicon – one at a time – until the tome's pages stop resembling pages at all. Until they become pure expurgatory-tangibull. Raven-striate leaves. Ebony reticulate sheets. Tenebrous night in thin tissue.

Contemnation by tissue! It is almost unbearable.

Am I being morose? I'm sorry. I cannot help it. I want you here. I cannot say how much.

Write me. Will I receive your letter? I can only hope.

I miss you so.

Love,
Tassie

A * C * E * GHI * * LMNOP * RSTUVWXY *

Th* *uic* *r*wn *ox *umps ov*r the la*y **g

My Nate,

Mannheim has come through! He has at least met the goal I wrote you concerning in my last letter: he has come up with a sentence 44 letters in length containing all the necessary 26 appearances. With the recent spate in migrations to the States, there is now a shortage: not nearly enough six- to seven-year-youngs to write the sentences. Conveniently, though, Mannheim is papa to an intelligent six-year-young lass – Paula – who met with success in her initial attempt at transcription. I cannot, alas, mail it to you, as I then put yours-truly at peril. (Only were I a youngster, six or seven, might I attempt to courier via the post such a precarious missive.) Perhaps it will somehow reach you through other means.

In other news: (Yes, there is much other news to tell!) Someone is relaying threats to the Council. Each counciliteur has gotten a copy: "Cease the insanity or you will perish." As a result, the – I must now call them what I am only too happy to call them: police goons – the police goons have gone house-to-house in their investigation, yet have yet to turn up anyone except the usual suspects – that is, virtually everyone on the isle not in Nollopian Cult thrallage. That isn't all: the Council has put crepuscular-to-auroric house arrest upon all Nollop civilians not in league with the cult.

Almost all the villagers, Mother tells me, are leaving – either moving to Town or to the States. She says that it's nearly a ghost town up there now. As there are no more customers, the store is no longer open. This is all right, though, she says; victuals were starting to run scarce. Soon she will have to come to town as well, to move into my Aunt Gwenette's house. (At least I will get to see her again. I truly miss her.) Uncle Amos, I am sorry to say, is no longer with us. There was a harsh exchange, Aunt Gwenette unhappy with his return to the alcoholic spirits! Now he lives with Uncle Isaac across town. Soon he will resolve one way or another – to leave or not to leave the isle.

Yes, that is now the topic on every lip. This salient, impertinent, Hamlettian choice.

To leave or not to leave.

To waive claim to our homes. To renounce our mother soil. To give up everything to those who warrant only our lowest contempt – to those who aspire to reign in outright tyranny, who misperceive Nollopian thoughts in service to rapacious intentions. Can they not see that *we* see what is happening here? Are we to them only silent, witless nonessentials – prostrate irrelevancies to step over in their march to own, to expropriate, to steal everything in sight – even our very tongues!

Nate, I have to tell you something important. I wasn't going to; however, it seems crucial to me now that you have a true, complete account as to what is going on here.

I wrote the letters. The ones with the threats. Were anyone to learn this, it will mean my ruin, perhaps even my execution.

(Smuggler-courier: my very existence is in your palms!)

I love you, Nate. I miss you greatly.

Tassie

PS. The Mephistophelians live here. Not in the Orient. You will get my meaning later.

Six big devils from Japan quickly forgot how to waltz.

Mrs. Mittie,

Help us.

Please. Something appalling has put my son Timmy in harm's way. The school says that he is eight. The school says he was eight last month. Since last month he has not given any care to what he says. He thought – we all thought – that he was exempt. That his exemption continues until Novemgroogy 13, when he turns eight. When he truly, legally turns eight. It seems that someone at the Village Archives got it wrong. Unless we can prove otherwise Timmy will have to leave Nollop. We haven't the necessary papers to prove our claim. We lost our last home, you see, lost everything in it to Hurricane Elspeth. Perhaps you might go to the school – might locate something to prove that Timmy won't turn eight until Novempoopy 13; thus Council proclamata cannot in any legal sense apply to him. Otherwise he will have to go!

We implore you.

Sincerely,
Georgeanne Towgate

Mrs. Towgate,

I went to the school. With my erstwhile colleague Miss Greehy's assistance I spent the morning searching all the papers pertaining to your son. I must relay that nothing that might help your case came to our attention.

I am truly sorry.

Sincerely,
Mittie Purcy

PS. The tempera picture on your letter's verso is really lovely. I am partial to seascapes; it will gain a choice spot on my wall.

Sweet, sweet Mittie,

I have ghastly news. They have Tassie. She awaits trial as suspect in those recent anonymous threats to the Council. Come as soon as you can. In the event there is a guilty ruling, expulsion will not constitute a legally punitive option. Such a ruling will only result in something much, much worse. Something I venture not even to say.

Gwenette

Gwenette, loving spouse,

Ella, my Ella,

A slip-up near a police goon. Now only minutes away: a rap on the portal, then a hasty trip to Pier Seven. Will I see you two prior to my leave? I'm sorry to hear the news concerning Tassie. Who is her lawyer? Are they even allowing her counsel? I might suggest someone. There isn't much time, though.

Will you see me go, or will you remain at the Correctional Center with Tassie? I will neglect something, I am sure. Without your help. What a help you have –

Enough!

I simply can't do it anymore. And why should I? Why be so careful now? Moments away from transportation to the dreaded "Pier of Goodbyes." What's the point? What is there left to lose?

Like a retarded robot I go into the pre-programmed mode, placing my brain on high-alert to avoid these Nollop-frowned-upon devil letters. The devils aren't in Japan! The devils are here. Satan is alive and well, right here in all his z-q-j-d-k-f-b, jumpy-brown-fox-slothful-pooch-quick-and-the-dead-glory – right here upon this devil's island of hatred and anger and unconscionable, inconsolable loss.

Hide this letter. Hide it well, but let me say the things that I must say. Before it's too late. Let me say that I love you both dearly. Let me say that I am so very sorry for returning to strong drink, for turning my back on you when you needed me most. Now that I have a voice, there are hundreds of other things I want to say. But cannot. Look into my heart and know them all.

And find it in your own hearts to forgive me.

You don't have to see me off. I know you're worried about Tassie. Be there with her, for her. But if you do come, please do me a small favor – a large favor, really. I'm not able to transport my miniature moonshine jugs to the pier. I would like to take them with me, though. You know that where I'm going they will be as good as money. You'll find them in my studio – stored together – all ten dozen of them. Half that number should suffice. Put them in one of the little crates; they'll be easier to convey that way.

Would you mind doing this one last thing for me? Pack my box with five dozen liquor jugs?

Thank you.

Be well. Be safe.

Until we meet again.

Your loving husband and father,
Amos

HIGH COUNCIL

Sunshine, Octonary 22

Notice to all Nollopians,

At precisely 12:00 tomorrow morning the letter "C" will cease to exist at all points on this isle. You will eschew its use or receive penalties as per earlier Council proclamata. We note that a "u" is gone as well. Its twin, however, remains intact.

Sincerely,
Hamilton
Executive Secretary
Nollop High Council

A***E*GHI**LMNOP*RSTUVWXY*

Th* *ui** *r*wn *ox **mps ov*r the la*y **g

Mrs. Mittie,

I value, nonetheless, your going to the learny-house to help my son. Little Timmy values it as well.

He is gone now. Timmy. This morning. With Nash, my spouse. I must remain. I must remain, as I am without violation. Nash has two. One among us must stay. I am the one. Our home, our property – it's all that we have, you see. Were we all to leave, they will expropriate it. They expropriate property, you're aware, are you not?

Please exonerate me. In your heart. I am so sorry that I was the one to report your violations. I'm so sorry that I was to learn what is truly important in our lives too, too late.

Write me as well. When time permits. I am the last one on my street. It gets so still, so lonely here at night. Eerily still. Anguishingly lonely. Not, though, when the L.E. goons motor through – their horns wailing. Hooligans. As a rule, though, it is ghostly silent here.

How are you set with rations? I will soon have to miss one meal every sun-to-sun. Are you giving thought to moving to Town?

I may wish to go with you.

Write soon.
Georgeanne Towgate

PS. The painting was mine. It pleases me that you wish to hang it in your home! I will paint you more.

Wetty, Onomatopoeia 25

Mrs. Mittie,

Where are you? You are not home when I go to your portal. When I ring, I note no movement within your house. Have you gone to Town? Have you gone to the States?

I am apprehensive. Am I now alone?

Georgeanne

Sweet Tassie,

They will not let me into the prison to see you. I have spent the entire postnoon, all the early hours ensuing my arrival in town, waiting. Waiting here on the prison's visitors' lawn to see you.

Waiting.

Waiting.

They tell us nothing. (Will they even give this letter to you?) It is very upsetting. I want you to grasp how greatly I love you. I won't try to learn why you sent the threats. They push us all to the point where we say things, operate in ways that are not at all as we really are.

Were anything to happen to you, what then?

With all my love,
Mother

To Tassie's Mother Mittie,

My guess is that you are now with your sister, so I am routing this letter to her house. I am here in Nollop. (A stowaway, an illegal alien. I have spent the last 24 hours in nail-nipping intrigue!) All to see the one I love. To help the one I love. I am aware that they have put her in prison, though she will not stay there long. I will see to it. Wish me well.

Truly yours,
Nate

NOLLOPTON
Sunshine, O Tempora! 29

Ella,

While you were at the prison, attempting with your Aunt Mittie yet again to get in to see Tassie, men who were sent here to see me got themselves into our own sorry impregness with little struggle at all. Apparently, they were sent to interrogate me – the grilling pertaining to the now exanimate anti-high-priestal movement. Unhappy with my initial responses, they grew instantly perpy when I soon let slip an illegal letter. What enormous toothy grins! What mouth-enamel! You see, I gave them reason to transport me. To Pier Seven. Toss me right onto the emigrant trawler. No more Mum. One less agitator. (I am an agitator!) My leave happens very soon. As soon as I am through with this epistle to you.

It's a weeping shame. Why, I am not even given enough time to gather my things! All my possessions, your Pop's possessions are yours now, I suppose. Preserve them. Preserve our memory. I wish you to stay. You *must* stay.

Maintain the struggle. In our name. In our honor.

(I am so sorry that they will not permit me to see you prior to weighing moor. Give your Aunt Mittie a huge hug with my name on it. Tassie, as well.)

Until we meet again, sweet Ella.

With love always,
Your Mum

Mother, Ella:

You two must stop whiling your postnoons near the prison gates. They will not let you in to see me. Go now. There are things to attain elsewhere. You're aware, right? The things I mean?

Love,
Tassie

(This is the last time I will terminate a letter in this manner now that "V" is soon to leave us. A new letter goes. So what else is new?)

A***E*GHI**LMNOP*RSTU*WXY*

Th* *ui** *r*wn *ox **mps o**r the la*y **g

[Slipped under the Minnow Pea front door]

NOLLOPTON PRISON
NOLLOPTON
Toes (Halloween), Oompahpah 31

Miss Pea:

Man was here. Young man. Southern U.S. While you were home. Got your relation. Got your Aunt. I let him get that Tassie – that angel girl – let him steal her, pure truth! I must sign paper saying this – per authorities. They were here – the authorities. They put me to signing this paper saying what happen.

Anyway, you got no reason to return to this prison anymore. Seeing that she is no longer here. They will put eye to your house, though. Might they show up there – Tassie-girl, your aunt, young Ameri-man. My guess, though, is that those three are gone-gone – set sail I'm sure to the States. Anyway, this is the thing: you no got to return.

Guess what? I go to the lash. A sentry who lets a prisoner go, he gets the lash, gets the whole nine-tail-lam. It's worth it, though. To see that sweet, pretty girl release! Hurrah!

Yours truly,
Sentry William P.

Ella –

I am no longer in prison. Nate is the reason. He got us (Mother, me). We are on our way to the States. My horseman-gallant in shining armor! I wish you were with us. Then again, it is important too that you remain in Nollop. Now rests almost solely upon you Enterprise 32. You will triumph, we are sure. Our hearts, our prayers are with you.

Tassie

PS. I am trusting that the young shrimper we met in the north lagoon will get this letter to you. He was on his way to Nollopton to sell his haul. As a result, this letter may smell slightly shrimpish.

NOLLOPTON
Wetty, Nosegay 1

Woman in pretty orange hat:

My name is Ella. I saw you yesters, rummaging in the rear –
that shut Italian restaurant on Main. No got to rummage. There
are plenty eats in Wally's store at Eighth meets Elm. (Are you a
shrimp eater?) Wally, I hear, is a humane man. He is rationing eats
– they will last longer this way. No money? No got to worry. We
who are still here will help one another. I want to meet you. See
me tonight?

I use to possess relations – my mother, my papa, my Aunt
Mittie, her she-heir Tassie. Gone now. All those near to me, gone.

I am alone. Perhaps you are alone too?

See me tonight? My home: 4 houses east. I got stew tomatoes!

Ella

NOLLOPTON
Thirsty, Notaphily 2

Ella,

Happy to get your letter. We possess a sense sometimes we are the only ones still here. We will see you not tonight. Tomorrow night, yes? I insist, though: my home. Little one – Penny – she is ill. She perhaps not so ill tomorrow, although she ought to stay in a little longer. We were not rummaging, we must say. We thought there was gas. Must get gas into our generator. How is your power? They supply us only one hour in the morning now. No one remaining at the power plant to man operations there.

Wally is a humane man, you are right. He is helping us in this trying time. We must all help one another.

Tanya T.
(the woman in the pretty orange hat)

Tanya,

What a sweet time I was shown at your house last night! It was so pleasant meeting your spouse. It was a pleasure too, meeting your girl Penny. I am happy that she is nearly well.

I was also happy to meet Mannheim, also his young assistant Tom, although not please to learn that the institute is no longer open. Nothing is open any more, is this true? Tom tells me that the state operates now only to relate the next letters to omit. There are no other magisterial assertions. The thug-uglies arrest, thrash – then expel. The high priests generate their alpha-elisions, then return to their lairs to eat what tasties were put there, while praying to Nollop, paying homage to Nollop, stooping, pros- trating, salaaming to Nollop. Ignoring all humanity in their Nollop-apotheosis.

Let us say Nollop *were* all-hallow preeminent Omnipotentate, why – still – shut out all those with whom one shares this planet? Were we put here on this earth only to worship? Exalting Nollop is to erase all that is non-Nollopian upon this isle. To utterly erase an upright, meritorious people. Genoerasure.

Oh the humanity!

So, tea tomorrow? I eagerly await your response.

Ella

PS. 43! 43! One step nearer our goal. I hope that Tom was all right with that hug.

My girl wove six dozen plaid
jackets before she quit.

Miss Pea,

A pleasure it was to meet you two nights ago. Your smile warms me, illuminating the gloom. (The hug was pleasant as well.)

We are alone at the institute now – Mannheim, his girl Paula, yours-truly. The entryways are hasp-shut; though we easily mount the trellis next to our lunette to gain entry. We then may toil on, without espy-ation. The other pupils – the other worthy assistants – they are, alas, all gone.

Expulsion.

None, I am happy to say, went willingly.

We, Miss Pea, (may I appell you Ella?) are the only ones who persist now in Enterprise 32. The others who remain on this isle plow their energies into hunting aliments, into maintaining shelter in these unsure, austere times. As a people, we Nollopians now seem to exist only elementally. Outright primals we are now!

Piteous loss.

A loss, though, that I may not examine too long as my mission shouts my name. *Our* mission. We are true partners in this.

May I also note that you are pleasingly pretty? (I let that slip out, I am sorry! I meant it, though!)

Mannheim's girl Paula will rap on your portal soon. She will present our latest attempt. There is little time. 11 sun-to-suns. Then the 16th.

"U" is gone. I suppose you're aware. The 1st aeiouy to go. Up until now the other graphemes were not aeiouys. When the aeiouys start to go, Ella, writing to you turns exponentially more grueling. I will not throw in the towel, though. I trust that you won't either. I truly relish our partnership.

Perhaps we may sup together tomorrow night at the uni-learnity? I will show you how to shinny up the trellis.

I got lime gelatin!

Your ally,
Tom

A***E*GHI**LMNOP*RST**WXY*

Th* **i** *r*wn *ox **mps o**r the la*y **g

NOLLOPTON
Monty, Nostromo 6

Hello there.

I am Ella – the one who smile at y'all yesters. Whose home is near. I am writing to people who are still here. Who I still see in the streets, who peep at me – wall-in, porthole, portiere people. Wanting to say something, with anxiety stilling erstwhile galloping yammers. It is important that we say something to one another – any little thing. We are not low-tier animals. We are higher entities, am I right? Say something. A greeting. Anything.

It is important, as well, that we stay in nearness to one another – not only in the proximital sense – in the sense also as persisters – inheritors. We are all that remains – the ones who maintain the remnants – the Nollop that earlier was.

Retreat is not an option.

Ella

NOLLOPTON
Monty, No-way 6

Insane woman name Ella:

Retreat is what we want. Go away. Let we alone.

Anonymess

NOLLOPTON
Monty, Nostomania 6

Mittie –

This letter I post on this here portal in hopes that Mittie might see it. That Mittie is staying here at her sister's home now. I hope hope hope it is so. I am in a home not too remote. Three homes away. It was empty when I got here. It is *my* home now.

It was a long trip – 2 night-to-nights – to get here on shoe – to get to where my ally Mittie perhaps is. I ate twigs. I slept in sewer-arroyos. The yellow-sphere shone harshly on me. In the north I was near insanity. It wasn't pretty.

Isolate. Solitary. So lonely it was where I was. More so lonely than here. Here where Mittie is!

Please ignore not my appeal. As earlier. When one moment Mittie was there, the next she was not. I am so sorry as I mention earlier, the things that I perpetrate to harm Mittie. What I see now – it's all so plain, my past errors so apparent to me now. I saw into the glass swarthy; yea, now my eyes are open!

I want eagerly to go to my Nash, to my son Timmy in the States. I may not. I am to stay here. Nash tells me this is how I am to help those I esteem – the only way to retain what little we own. Yet it is hopeless, my staying there in that remote hamlet where we possess the tiny property. What is the worth? Why is my staying there more important than seeing the ones I esteem: my Nash, my sweet, little, not-yet-eight-no-matter-what-anyone-says Timmy? Mittie sees, right? How I so miss my sweet ones!

We help one another now, agree? I say I am sorry; Mittie says it is all right. Mittie assents to this, yes? Please say we are mates.

Amigas. Say, please, that we are womanpals. I so greatly wish to hear these terms!

Georgeanne Towgate

(All letters still here! Yea!)

Georgeanne Towgate,

My mother's sister – the one thee wants – is gone. She went with her she-heir Tassie to the States. Tassie was in prison. The reason: she sent threats to the High Priests. They arrest her. She is happily no longer there. Alas, neither is the one thee wants.

This is, permit me to relate, why it was important that she exit thy hamlet so hastily. Not the one thee imagines. There was no ill will.

I shall sign on this moment as Georgeanne's ally! See, I am at times lonely too.

We eat together tonight, yes? Two lonely amigas.

I am eighteen. Yet my age is not important. Nothing is important next to Enterprise 32. I await thee.

Ella

Tom –

Here's the news: there is a new woman on my street. Her name is Georgeanne Towgate. She is lonely, shows great apprehension. I will try to help her. She is not at all similar to my Tom who is strong, wise, pleasing to the eye. Thy gelatin was so tasty. I am happy I met thee.

Ella

Ella,

No more gelatin nights now. Happy to report Enterprise 32 progress:

37! That's right: 37! Hip hip hooray!

It is all too awesome! Now only 5 to go. I will not sleep tonight. Neither will Mannheim.

Thy amigomate Tom

Zelda quickly wove eight nubby flax jumpers.

Tewstay, Nophemger 7

Greetings, Nollopians,

This is to inphorm ewe oph Statoot 28-63 past this morning with implorment phrom high elter R. Lyttle. Hensephorth, sitisens may – in graphy only – espress themselphs when warrant, threw yoose oph proxy letters, yet only as hear-twins. Any attempt to employ hear-twin graphemes in orality will warrant the most sepheerest penalties yonter the law.

Is this what Mr. Nollop woot want? On this, we are not sertin. Howepher, ewe may write to one another in this manner, ontil we rool otherwise.

Sinserely,
Hamilton Phergewson

Tewstay, Nophemger 7

Ella,

Yesters we open this portal to a Mr. M who was employ with the Penta-priests. He was let go – phyrt. Lost his apartment in gophermental homeplex. He has tales to tell, Ella. There are loonies – paranoi's at the helm! Intoxi-tipsy on raw, intemperate power. 2 oph the 5 seem to worry little what Nollop's wishes are. So entirely at ease they are with the power Nollop soppositely grant them. 2 others, tho, are the total opposite: monastian hermits – lashing one another with relish-whips when either oph them ephen things apowt a sin-letter.

It seems that Lyttle alone remains in possession oph his sanity.

Other news: last night my sister's man was stanting pheneath the senotaph when a new tile plonge. The tile with the letter X. It hit him right on his het. The priests are there pronto pronto to get the tile. They see my sister's man lying there, eyes not open. They gather the tile peeses. They stroll away, not ephen looging at him. Totally ignoring ingert man.

He meant nothing to them.

Later, help appears. A woman. She ministers to him, transports him home.

He was *nothing* to them, Ella.

Imagine that!

Yor neighper ant phrent Tanya

PS. I was apowt to post this letter when I hear: 3 more tiles plommet: a "T," an "R," an "H." Another "T" remains in plase. Another "R" ant another "H" as well. Ella may wish to no, tho, that essept phor "O" there are no more twins. The remaining letters are all singletons.

A * * * E * GHI * * LMNOP * RST * * W * Y *

T** **i** ***wn *o* **mps o**r *he la*y **g

To Miss Ella Minnow Pea:

I regret to tell yew most greephos news: Mannheim is mort. I no that yew new him, were phrents with him. That yew ant he ant his assistant Tom were worging still on the Enterprise 32 shallenge. How it happen is not easy to tell: he yoose an illegal letter in interphew aphter poleese see him ant Tom going threw wintow into yew-niphersity hall – trespassing. He yoose the letter, then when the poleese go to tie his hants to transport him to Pier 7, he ant Tom try to phlee so teportation will not happen.

The poleese shoot him. They shoot him in the het.

He is immetiately tet.

I am, again, sorry to tell yew this. I most say, tween we two, that I helt high hopes phor his sassess.

Yors trewly,
R. Lyttle

PS. As phor Tom – I am not sher what has happent to him. He phlet ant is perhaps in hyting.

To Mr. Lyttle,

Thangs 4 telling me oph what happen to Mr. Mannheim. Yew are right. We were inteet worging together. A phrentship was growing among we three, as well. It is hart 4 me to ephen write, I am so staggert phrom this news. He was a goot man who sherisht this islant with all his hart. I will miss him. I will miss as well his teephotion to Enterprise 32. I am not sertin I possess the strength to persepheere withowt him.

Yew were sossessphill in getting the – whatepher yor naming yorselphs now – to pass Statoot 28-63. Why not tern all yor energy to opher-terning all the hanoss lipogrammata statoots? Restoring this islant its tignity?

I haph not hert phrom Tom. I am worriet apowt his sayph-tee.

Sinserely,
Ella

To Ella Minnow Pea,

Yew are solisiting the impossiple, Miss Pea. Shirley yew no that now. I soggest yew get to worg. Mannheim woot want it this way.

Insitentally, I will let ewe no iph yong Tom appears.

Sinserely,
R. Lyttle

To Ella Minnow Pea,

I haph Pawla Mannheim with me – orphant, yoo no, aphter what happent to her phather, Prophessor Mannheim. She is with me temporarily. Howepher, she may not stay past tomorrow. She has no other relatiphs to go to, not here or in the States. I haph too many other phoster yooths to tent to.

So I am senting her to yoo.

Sinserely,
Marigolt Shropshire

Early Phrytay morning

Ella –

I am alyph ant well. Please tont worry apowt me. I haph mate this one phirtiph mitnight phoray to leaph this note. As mosh as I wish to see ewe ant ontill this nightmare is opher, I may not again emerge phrom my phewgitiph's hyting plase. Enterprise 32 is all yors now. Gott grant ewe the strength to see it to its phinish.

Yor phrent,
Tom

Tanya,

I was sent letter phrom a Marigolt Shropshire. I am new phostermother 4 Mannheim's girl Pawla! Apparently, there are no other relatiphs 4 her to go to.

It is a strange worlt we resite in, is it not? I am mate a phoster mother at eighteen! I will try to giph her a goot home. Poor little raggamophin!

How is Georgeanne? I haph not seen or hert phrom her 4 a while. I am a little worreet.

Ella

Ella,

Tanya toll me yew were assing aphter me. I am phine.

Lately, I haph startet painting my torso in pretty, motley hews. I sit in phront oph the mirror in the sleepy-room. I atmire my hantyworg. I am a hooman apstrat painting!

This morning I got some olt remnant paint phrom the hartware warehoose. Now I haph enoph to paint all opher my whole selph!

Yor phrent,
Georgeanne

To Georgeanne,

It isn't wise 4 a person to paint her whole selph. Thing apowt this phirst. Yew will see that it is not healthy. Also, please answer yor portal when I rap.

Ella

Ella –

I loog 4 yew all aphternoon. Yew are, I thing, at Mrs. Shropshire's home getting little Pawla's things together. I toog Georgeanne to the hospital. There is one physisian still worging there, thang Gott!

Georgeanne is phery ill with let poisoning. There is a possipility that she may not last the night.

Loog 4 me at the hospital tonight when yew see this note.

Also, yew hear that "Y" phell? No "Y" tomorrow. At least no one was hert this time.

Trooly yors,
Tanya (tomorrow: "Tanea")

A * * * E * G H I * * L M N O P * R S T * * W * * *

T** **i** ***wn *o* **mps o**r *he la** **g

To Mr. Little: ("Little" is permissaple now, no? Let me no iph ewe prepher some other name in its stet.)

Mie phrent Georgeanne perisht last night phrom let poisoning. I thing, also she was not right in the het. I most write to her phamilee. Mie other phrent Tanea tells me this morning that she along with her phamilee are leaphing Nollop to go to the States.

She will transport Georgeanne's remains to the Towgate phamilee. Tanea also wants Pawla – Mannheim's little girl. She pheels Nollop is a wastelant now, no plase 4 a little girl. No plase 4 aneeone 4 that matter. I will not stop her. It is goot to get her awae phrom here.

I hartlee got to no Little Pawla. We might haph mate goot phrents.

I pheel as Georgeanne most haph when epheree-one lepht the willage. Alone. Phorsaagen.

Are ewe leaphing too, Mr. Little? Will Mr. Little soon wipe his hants oph all this tragi-mess? Tern on his heel – tisappear?

Ella

OPHIS OPH R. LITTLE
NOLLOPTON
Montae, Nophemger 13

Ella,

Ewe mae repher to me as "Little." I am repherring to miselph that wae now.

To answer the interrogatoree, I haph no plans to leaph this isle. Espeshellee sinse I haph goot reason to remain.

Ewe see, I am worging on Enterprise 32 mie-selph.

As, I hope, are ewe.

In these three son-to-sons that remain – this "last lap" as it were – I thot ewe might appresiate the help.

Sinserelee,
R. Little

To the Towgate Phamilee:

Please asept mie hartphelt simpathee at this time. Georgeanne passt awae last night phrom let poisoning. She paintet her whole selph phrom het to toe with manee prettee, ornamental hews. She was so resplentent, almost ratiant in repose – the happee, appealing pigments an aesthetit reminter oph her lophlee warm spirit.

She shoot loog smashing 4 the phooneral.

Her remains shoot arriph shortlee.

With all regrets,
Ella Minnow Pea

Ella,

Pharewell. Pharewell. Tho we were not phrents 4 long, I will so miss ewe. Ewe are strong. It is goot that ewe are lepht. We wish ewe well with Enterprise 32. We wish ewe well with ephereething ewe trie to asheeph in these trieing phinal taes. To asheeph 4 Nollop. 4 all we espatriot Nollopians. The Nollopian tiaspora!

Aphetionatelee,
Tanea ant phamilee

PS. "H" has phallen. (Hee hee, ho ho. How totallee irrelephant to mie lieph now!)

A * * * E * G * I * * LMNOP * RST * * W * * *

T** **i** ***wn *o* **mps o**r **e la** **g

To: Mr. Warren
Nollopiana
Georgia
Ameriga

Mr. Warren,

Please get wort to mie Momma, to mie Pop ant to Mittie ant Tassie tat I am well. I am a persister, an ootlaster. No more trepitation 4 me. Onlee tetermination!

Tetermination to ent tee tast I startet. Tee otts are not goot. Tee reason: *I* am not goot. Manneim was saperior to me. Ant Assistant Tom. Now Manneim is tet, ant Tom is – I no not ware. All *I* am is present. Positioning, stringing letters togeter. 26 into 32. Ontill tee time rons owt. Ontill it all stops.

Ontill ... silense.

Ontill ... Nollop is no more.

No more.

Alto I no tat Nollop isn't trewlee going awae. Tee reason: *I* am not going awae. I will learn to tawg in noomerals. I will learn sign langwage – anee-ting to stae in Nollop. I, Mr. Little, ant tee sparse-peoples still strolling Nollop's santee, saltee-air seasite, gaseing at sonrises too glorios to plase into worts – we will possess tease tings alwaes! Nollop troo also in ower memories – teep, teep witin ower soles.

I miss ewe all teeplee. I am sorree to atmit, Momma, tat I am presentlee a snoop! I reat letters – teer, sweet letters ewe wrote to Pop – warm, engaging letters Pop wrote to ewe. Some olt, some new, all ewe gesst no one woot see – ewe pot tem awae so well! I reat tem, ewe see, to gain neetet inspiration.

Teese letters are also mie solass. Mie emollient!

Ant I tang ewe 4 tem.

Insitentallee, ewe are propaplee reating mie last letter to ewe. It is now simplee too tiring to write. To sae watt I most sae in lang-wage one mae onterstant.

I am so sorree.

Alwaes,
Ella

Nollopians:

G go tonite at mitnite. No more "G." So long "G."

Penta-priests

A * * * E * * * I * * LMNOP * RST * * W * * *

T** **i** ***wn *o* **mps o**r **e la** ***

Letter to me:

Onlee 24 owers remain.

Storm.

Tiles plop. 8 tiles plomp plomp all in one nite.

Tee ent is near.

So lon A!

So lon E! (Nise to no ewe.)

So lon I!

So lon R! (Are ewe lonesome tonite?)

So lon S!

So lon T!

So lon W!

So lon O twin. (Remnant-twin is all alone now.)

Now onlee 5 remain at 12 o'time. Onlee 5. Onlee 5 remain.

Wear is tat paint?

Sinserelee,
Ella

************LMNOP************

*** ***** ****n *o* **mp* **** *** |*** ***

"LMNOP":

No mo Nollop pomp!

No mo Nollop poo poo!

No mo 4 pop/1 moll Nollop looloo poop!

No no no mo plop, plop, plop, plomp!

No mo Nollop!

No, mon, no! O Nooooooo!

OOOOOOOOOOOOOOOOOOOOOOOOOOOOOOOOO
OOOOOOOOOOOOOOOOOOOOOOOOOOOOOOOOO!

— *"LMNOP"*

... Put them in one of the little crates; they'll be easier to convey that way.

Would you mind doing this one last thing for me?

Pack my box with five dozen liquor jugs?

Thank you.

Be well. Be ...

P**A**ck my box with five dozen liquor jugs?

Pack my **B**ox with five dozen liquor jugs?

Pa**C**k my box with five dozen liquor jugs?

Pack my box with five **D**ozen liquor jugs?

Pack my box with fiv**E** doz**E**n liquor jugs?

Pack my box with **F**ive dozen liquor jugs?

Pack my box with five dozen liquor ju**G**s?

Pack my box wit**H** five dozen liquor jugs?

Pack my box w**I**th f**I**ve dozen l**I**quor jugs?

Pack my box with five dozen liquor **J**ugs?

Pac**K** my box with five dozen liquor jugs?

Pack my box with five dozen **L**iquor jugs?

Pack **M**y box with five dozen liquor jugs?

Pack my box with five doze**N** liquor jugs?

Pack my b**O**x with five d**O**zen liqu**O**r jugs?

Pack my box with five dozen liquor jugs?

Pack my box with five dozen li**Q**uor jugs?

Pack my box with five dozen liquo**R** jugs?

Pack my box with five dozen liquor jug**S**?

Pack my box wi**T**h five dozen liquor jugs?

Pack my box with five dozen liq**U**or j**U**gs?

Pack my box with fi**V**e dozen liquor jugs?

Pack my box **W**ith five dozen liquor jugs?

Pack my bo**X** with five dozen liquor jugs?

Pack m**Y** box with five dozen liquor jugs?

Pack my box with five do**Z**en liquor jugs?

ABCDEFGHIJKLMNOPQRSTUVWXYZ

Pack my box with five dozen liquor jugs

NOLLOPTON
Thursday, November 16

Dear Mr. Rederick Lyttle,

Here is the sentence you require, delivered prior to the deadline imposed by the High Council – indeed, with three whole hours to spare.

Pack my box with five dozen liquor jugs.

Please note that this sentence is exactly 32 letters in length. It contains the requisite appearances of each of the 26 letters of the English alphabet. The sentence contains, further, no contractions or arguable proper names. It is, incidentally, neither declarative nor interrogative, but, in fact, is in the imperative mood. It is a command, Mr. Lyttle. An appropriate response to fifteen weeks of High Council orders, mandates, and edictal behests.

I must inform you that I did not come up with the sentence myself. The credit should actually go to my father Amos Minnow Pea. If, indeed, credit is due. I maintain that because the sentence was created unintentionally, in the course of a quickly penned farewell letter to my mother and me, Pop should not own responsibility. Nor should anyone. Or, perhaps, all of us.

And this is why I venture to tell you the truth of its genesis, risking, of course, a strict interpretation of your challenge. I venture so, for this reason, Mr. Lyttle: any one of us could have come up with such a sentence. We are, when it comes right down to it, all of us: mere monkeys at typewriters. Like Nollop. Nollop, low order primate elevated to high order ecclesiastical primate, elevated still further in these darkest last days to ultimate prime A grade superior being. For doing that which my father did without thinking. Think about it.

Truly yours,
Ella Minnow Pea

FROM THE OFFICE OF HIGH COUNCILMAN
REDERICK LYTTLE

Thursday, November 16
(Day One of the New Order)

Dear Miss Minnow Pea:

On behalf of the High Council, I accept your sentence. All relevant statutes have been rescinded. Please join me at your earliest convenience for tea in my office. I trust that your friend Tom, after having been successfully flushed out, will accompany you.

Fondly,
Rederick Lyttle

Dear Mum, Pop, Mittie, and dear cousin Tassie,

It is over. You may all come home. Mr. Lyttle, on behalf of the High Council, has accepted my sentence – the thirty-two-letter sentence which I proffered three hours prior to deadline. The council members assembled to read it, assembled in one great bug-eyed clump to read it aloud – over and over – then proceeded to examine it most carefully, counting each letter, identifying and pronouncing each grapheme in proper alphabetical sequence, and finally proclaiming the sentence an undeniable miracle.

It is not a miracle. It is an accident. Pure happenstance. Perhaps just as happenstantial in its creation as was the fox/dog sentence. I have strong reason to believe this. Let me tell you why.

This morning Mr. Lyttle took Tom (my new friend – I cannot wait for you to meet him; the intense blue of his eyes gives me occasional shudders!) and me down into the vault beneath the national library. Held in climate-controlled perpetuity are several hundred linear feet of government records and historical documents, including the original Island Compact which we have all gazed upon in its infrequent public displays, along with a sizeable collection of Mr. Nevin Nollop's personal papers and most private effects. I asked Mr. Lyttle why all of this was spared in the wake of the anti-alphabetical edicts which had rendered to dust and ash virtually everything else found in print upon this island. It seems that efforts were indeed underway to find masons to seal off the vault, entombing it behind a solid brick wall, burying as unintended time capsule, these immurement-destined remnants of a time when discourse came without stricture – without posthumous Nollopian challenges-cum-curses.

Among those papers Tom and I discovered a book – an amply illustrated children's storybook with Nollop's name scrawled in child-like letters upon the title page. The book told the tale of a dog who does not wish to participate in a fox hunt. A lazy dog who would go so far as to permit a fleet fox to leap directly overhead rather than lift a single paw to pursue him. In his juvenile hand Nollop had kid-crabbed the following: "Oh you lazy dog! The brown fox is so quick and you are so lazy. Bad dog! Bad dog!"

Of course, there are those who believe that Nollop was too stupid to concoct the national sentence from even these obvious elements. It could very well be that someone else wrote it, and he took full credit. I would not put it past him.

All the Council members save Lyttle have tendered their resignations. Immediately thereafter Harton Mangrove attempted suicide with his necktie. It was a clumsy attempt and quickly foiled. Following our excursion to the vault, Lyttle, Tom and I proceeded to the cenotaph, climbed to the top, and with sledgehammers in hand, initiated, in earnest, an act of destructive revisionism. Others among the few of us still left on the island jubilantly joined in. There followed a celebratory bonfire and weenie roast. We exercised our newly liberated vocabularies until dawn.

As we were all gathering for breakfast, courtesy of an early morning raid on the amply stocked Willingham family larder, we learned that Harton Mangrove had again tried to take his own life, this time by repeatedly whacking himself in the head with a heavy wooden rolling pin. He was left stunned on his kitchen floor by his wife and three young sons who were late for their seven a.m. slinkoff for Florida where they would soon be taking up permanent residency. Reports are in conflict as to what Mangrove mumbled as he lay dazed upon the floor, painfully clutching his lumpy head. One witness attested to the following: "I am floundering upon the shoals of despair, forsaken by the

Great and Powerful Nollop!" Another heard simply, "Somebody get me a headache powder. I think I juggled my brains!"

There were some among the survivors who wanted to erect a monument to me; others thought Pop, as the actual creator of the sentence that was to serve as vehicle for our emancipation, deserving of all the national approbation. I suggested that neither of us was an appropriate candidate given the fortuity of the sentence's conception. But this fact does not preclude the erection of some other concrete memorial to those who lost life, property, strips of dorsal epidermis, and/or sanity to the tyranny of the last four months. I suggested, further, that the following might be sculpted: a large box filled with sixty moonshine jugs – piled high, toppling over, corks popping, liquor flowing. Disorder to match the clutter and chaos of our marvelous language. Words upon words, piled high, toppling over, thoughts popping, correspondence and conversation overflowing.

And upon the bandiford beneath the sculpture, writ not on tiles, but chiseled deeply into the marble façade, the following sentence nineteen letters in length, containing a mere ten different graphemes of the English alphabet:

"Dead dogs tell no tails."

And by deliberately keeping the word "tails" frustratingly mishomonymized – we offer this guarantee: that our descendants will never have reason to exalt this sentence beyond simple sentience.

Finis.

I miss you all, and cannot wait to see you again.

Love,
Ella Minnow Pea

Dear Doug,

It's after the fact, obviously, but we're all still curious to know what you and your fellow cyber-geeks might have been able to come up with. Care to give it a shot? By way of reminder, your mission, should you choose to accept it:

Shortest possible sentence containing all twenty-six letters of the alphabet. Words in English, and in current usage, please. I'll accept proper names in a pinch, if they don't seem Martian.

Best wishes,
Nate ("the Scribbler") Warren

Dear Nate,

We have come up with four sentences for your reading pleasure, each equal to or less than 32 letters in length. Allowing for, thank you, sir, the use of proper names, the computer succeeded in creating a sentence exactly twenty-six letters in length, that is – need I say it – without repetition of a single letter. It follows:

J.Q. Vandz struck my big fox whelp.

The others we are pleased to list below:

Quick zephyrs blow, vexing daft Jim. (29)

Few quips galvanized the mock jury box. (32)

Pack my box with five dozen liquor jugs. (32)

I hope this has been of some help to you. What, by the way, was the sentence which brought the High Council to its senses (or shall we say, to its knees)? We're all quite curious to know.

Sincerely,
Doug (Cyber-head) Watts

The End